SHORT STORIES OF THE UNEXPECTED

Taking Flight

JACQUES SARDAS

Also by Jacques Sardas

Without Return: Memoirs of an Egyptian Jew 1930–1957

Taking Flight

Archway Publishing books may be ordered through booksellers or by contacting:

Archway Publishing
1663 Liberty Drive
Bloomington, IN 47403
www.archwaypublishing.com
844-669-3957

Because of the dynamic nature of the Internet, any web addresses or links contained in this book may have changed since publication and may no longer be valid. The views expressed in this work are solely those of the author and do not necessarily reflect the views of the publisher, and the publisher hereby disclaims any responsibility for them.

Any people depicted in stock imagery provided by Getty Images are models, and such images are being used for illustrative purposes only.
Certain stock imagery © Getty Images.

Adobe Stock images: 18: Glass Hat/stock.adobe.com; 60: jekatarinka/stock.adobe.com; 62: Sirapat/stock.adobe.com; 78: Adriana/stock.adobe.com; 87: nsit0108/stock.adobe.com; 118: inarik/stock.adobe.com

ISBN: 978-1-6657-5902-1 (sc)
ISBN: 978-1-6657-5901-4 (hc)
ISBN: 978-1-6657-5900-7 (e)

Library of Congress Control Number: 2024907617

Print information available on the last page

Archway Publishing rev. date: 07/02/2024

For my mother, Dora Beja Sardas—my hero—who dedicated her short life to raising and educating her four children under extremely stressful conditions; for all the mothers in my extended family; and for mothers the world over whose heroic deeds hold their families together

Contents

Introduction

One pleasant summer night in 2022, my wife, Etty, and I had dinner in the backyard of the home where one of our daughters lives with her husband. After the meal, our family, including our twenty-three-year-old granddaughter, Rachel, remained at the table chatting about all kinds of matters. As I sipped a glass of red wine, I mentioned to the group that I wanted to write a book of short stories—a departure for me, since the only book I had written prior to this was my memoir, a work of nonfiction.

In describing the stories, I think I used the word "weird." I didn't want to write anything run-of-the-mill . . . I wanted readers to be surprised and maybe even a little puzzled as they read. I wanted to give them something to wonder about. My stories would be quirky; different; odd.

Rachel seemed particularly enthusiastic about this idea. She jumped up from her chair, came over to my side of the table, and took my hand. "Please, please write your stories," she implored. "Do you promise?"

I held her hand and said yes. The evening was so comfortable, the dinner so delicious, and the wine so tasty. What else could I do? I agreed.

It took me a long time to start the project because I was busy—or at least that was the excuse I used at the time. The following year, though, at the approach of my ninety-third birthday, I finally sat down in front my computer and got cracking.

I had fun writing about Avi, whose life story somewhat parallels mine, and all the other scalawags and mavericks and nonconformists who populate my imagination and the pages of this book. May you have as much fun reading about them as I had in bringing them to life.

Timeline

Avi is born in Egypt

Ten years later: Avi's mother dies

Sixteen years later: Avi and Sara get married, then leave Egypt and immigrate to Brazil

One month later: Avi and Sara's daughter Rahel is born

One year later: Avi begins his career in sales at a large multinational firm headquartered in New York City

Three years later: Avi and Sara's daughter Hanna is born

Seven years later: Avi and Sara leave Brazil and immigrate to France; Avi becomes president of the multinational firm's French subsidiary

Seven years later: Avi and Sara leave France and immigrate to Israel; the firm promotes Avi to vice president in charge of the Middle East and Africa

Five years later: Avi and Sara leave Israel and immigrate to New York; Avi becomes president of the company

The Three Old Buddies

We were together again in Montevideo in December of 1999: Eddie, Moti, and me. We had decided to spend some time together, just the three of us, while our wives went shopping. The women preferred to go without us anyway so they could take their time and spend however much they wanted on whatever they wanted without the men looking over their shoulders.

It was also a good arrangement for us, the three old buddies. We could talk freely and tease one another as we used to when we were kids. It reminded us of the good old days.

The three of us had met in Cairo, at the Jewish Community School, when we were in fourth grade. Subsequently, we left Egypt during the "second exodus," which started in the late 1950s and culminated in the mid-1960s, the only way to escape Gamal Abdel Nasser's xenophobic edicts and persecution of the Jews. At one time, there were eighty thousand Jews living in Egypt, but only a handful remained, most too old, too tired, and too weak to leave.

Eddie, Moti, and I ultimately ended up in far friendlier and safer lands—Chile, Brazil, and the United States respectively. We had managed to build comfortable lives for ourselves: Eddie owned a department store in La Unión, a small city in southern Chile; Moti opened a factory in São Paulo specializing in tools for the cigarette industry; and I was enjoying a good career at a multinational corporation headquartered in New York City. Life was good. And even though we had kept our friendship alive during the previous sixty years with regular phone calls, emails, and in-person visits, we always looked forward to getting together with our wives once or twice a year for longer visits, especially during holidays and vacations. In December of 1999, we decided to spend time in Uruguay.

That afternoon in Montevideo, we were looking for a quiet place where we could have a drink and, as usual, reminisce about our childhoods in Egypt, relive the pranks we played on one another, and recall the scary and often hilarious adventures we had in our younger years.

We found a brasserie that had outdoor tables and sat down, ready to relax and catch up. Eddie was the one who chose the place. He was especially eager to chat, but Moti and I saw the familiar signs of his enthusiasm for weighty discussions of his favorite subjects, including the origin of the world, the existence or nonexistence of God, and current events. His cheeks were pink, and he seemed in a hurry.

No, Eddie was not interested in reminiscing: he had something he wanted to say.

He took a folded piece of paper from his back pocket and put on a pair of reading glasses. "In a couple of days," he began, looking at Moti and me over his glasses, "we are going to close this decade, start a new one, and welcome the third millennium."

Moti and I exchanged a furtive glance. *Where is he going with this?*

"Do you know how many people died and lost their homes just during the past decade as a result of natural disasters?"

With a theatrical gesture, Eddie snapped open the piece of paper and placed it on the table. He cleared his throat and started reading.

"In June of 1990, Iran was hit by the 7.4-magnitude Manjil-Rudbar earthquake. Tehran experienced catastrophic damage, and almost fifty thousand people lost their lives.

"Making landfall in April of 1991, the Bangladesh cyclone whipped up a twenty-foot storm surge that devastated the country's coastline, killing close to 139,000 people.

"In the early hours of September 30, 1993, the Indian state of Maharashtra was shaken by the Latur earthquake. Almost ten thousand people were killed, and many more were displaced.

"One of Japan's most populated cities, Kobe, was struck by the Great Hanshin Earthquake in January of 1995. An entire freeway collapsed, and four hundred thousand buildings were destroyed. Most horrific, however, was the more than six thousand lives that were lost.

"The category 5 Hurricane Mitch was one of the deadliest ever recorded. It struck Central America in late October of 1998. Honduras and Nicaragua got the worst of it: approximately eleven thousand people lost their lives, and millions of people were left homeless.

"And now we come to the disasters that occurred *this year alone*." Eddie paused. "The İzmit earthquake hit northwestern Turkey in August, causing a staggering seventeen thousand deaths. It was followed by a tsunami that killed 155 people.

"In late October, a deadly tropical cyclone struck India's eastern coast, battering the state of Odisha with 160-mile-an-hour winds. It took the lives of nine thousand people.

"After weathering torrential rainfall from successive storms just this month, Venezuela experienced its worst disaster in recorded history. The sheer volume of rain that fell during the Vargas tragedy destabilized the land and caused enormous mudslides, killing anywhere from ten thousand to thirty thousand people."

Eddie stopped, took off his glasses, and scrutinized us. "Do you realize that more than half a million people died as a result of these natural disasters?" He waited a few seconds, then took another piece of paper from his pocket and waved it in front of us. "And here is a series of murderous attacks against the Jews."

Putting on his glasses once more, he continued with his grim litany.

"On March 17, 1992, Hezbollah claimed responsibility for a blast that leveled the Israeli embassy in Buenos Aires, causing the deaths of twenty-nine people and wounding 242.

"On August 21, 1995, Hamas claimed responsibility for the detonation of a bomb that went off on a bus in Jerusalem, killing six people and injuring more than one hundred.

"On February 26, 1996, again in Jerusalem, a suicide bomber blew up another bus, killing twenty-six people and injuring some eighty more.

"On March 4, 1996, Hamas and the Palestine Islamic Jihad both claimed responsibility for a bombing outside Tel Aviv's largest shopping mall, the Dizengoff Center, which killed twenty and injured seventy-five.

"Then on September 4, 1997, three suicide bombers detonated bombs in the Ben Yehuda pedestrian mall in Jerusalem, killing eight and wounding nearly two hundred others."

Eddie put his papers back in his pocket and looked at us, awaiting our reaction. We shifted in our chairs, unable to meet his eyes.

Eddie leaned forward across the table. He growled, "These are people, human beings like us who died horrible deaths."

I was wondering what had happened to the nice, pleasant reunion we had planned.

Suddenly, Moti stood up and, in a mixture of Portuguese and French, shouted, "Deixa pra lá, tout ça—qui s'en fout?" (Let it go, all that—who cares?) "Deixa pra lá, tout ça—qui s'en fout?" he said again and again, moving his hips and arms in a kind of lazy samba. "Deixa pra lá, tout ça—qui s'en fout?"

Moti's song-and-dance show was funny and contagious. I couldn't resist. I stood up, put my arm around Moti's shoulder, and sang and danced with him.

Eddie was mortified. He held his face in his hands, as if he were trying to hide from the spectacle.

Moti and I went to Eddie and pulled him off his chair. "Come on, Eddie. We came here to have fun. For the sake of our sixty-year-long friendship, dance and sing with us. Deixa pra lá, tout ça—qui s'en fout? La vie est belle!"

Finally Eddie shuffled his feet and mumbled, "La vie est belle."

The three of us laughed loudly, just as we had as children.

I caught the waiter's eye. "Ola, mesero: tres grande cervezas bien heladas, por favor."

As soon as the waiter came back with the beers, we raised our glasses in a toast. "Qui s'en fout?" we cried. "Life is good!"

The Gambler

*I*t was the end of my first year at my first job after my high school graduation. I had just received an additional month's salary as a year-end bonus, and to celebrate, I persuaded my friend Eddie to accompany me to the Auberge des Pyramides.

The Auberge des Pyramides was Cairo's trendiest entertainment spot, a place only the rich and famous could afford. Its restaurant was the best in town, and its unique nightclub featured entertainment from Europe and Latin America.

But these were not the reasons I wanted to go to the Auberge. I wanted to go there to visit its casino, well known all over the world. King Farouk used to go there with other royals to have fun and lose some of the vast fortune he had amassed.

I wanted to gamble.

I had just finished reading Dostoyevsky's novel *The Gambler* and could not get it off my mind. I had read many of Dostoyevsky's books, but *The Gambler*—which he wrote in twenty-six days to satisfy a ruthless and unscrupulous creditor—seemed more real, more vivid than the others, maybe because it paralleled Dostoyevsky's own struggles with compulsive gambling.

Besides, I sympathized with Alexei, the main character: he was a nice, intelligent man, living from paycheck to paycheck with no prospect of a better future. Maybe I identified with him because I found myself in the same situation. Just once I wanted to feel the same rush of adrenaline, the same heightened anticipation Alexei felt at the roulette table. But win or lose, I knew I would only be a one-night gambler.

Early one Saturday evening, Eddie and I took a bus to downtown Cairo and from there a taxi to the Auberge des Pyramides. Eddie wore his best suit, and I wore the only suit I had. Fortunately, we were both presentable enough to be admitted by the Auberge's reception desk. I transferred some of the money I had brought to my jacket's inside pocket to make sure we had enough to get us back home. We were both excited and nervous.

To try to relax, we decided to spend some time walking around and admiring the casino's luxurious decor. We stopped at the baccarat table and watched older people in tuxedos and glittering evening gowns as they moved large stacks of chips back and forth across the felt surface. We stopped at the blackjack tables, where younger people were dressed more casually and bet more moderately.

We finally entered the largest and noisiest room in the casino, which contained the roulette tables. Like Alexei in *The Gambler*, I felt my stomach cramp when I heard the clicking of the chips and the bouncing of the ball against the wheel. My heart was thundering in my chest.

Eddie and I entered the room as inconspicuously as we could. In the process of choosing the table where I would play, I recalled Dostoyevsky's description of Alexei. I tried to guess who was the one who was most like him—the one who was betting his life and that of his loved one on the spin of the wheel.

Eddie and I exchanged our money for chips and chose separate tables. I wanted to be alone—alone with my emotions.

I decided to bet on the black 8, between the red 23 and red 30, because 8 was my number on my community basketball team, the Maccabi.

My first bets were shy, just warm-ups. But then I became more daring, hoping that the odds in my favor would increase the longer I played. Every time I lost, I increased my bet, sure that the little ball would stop at the number 8 on the next spin.

The urge to continue was irresistible. It never occurred to me to quit. I was certain I would win an enormous sum of money that I'd be proud to show to Eddie, my colleagues at work, and my basketball teammates.

But the number 8 proved elusive. Meanwhile, the pile of chips in front of me was getting smaller. At last I put my remaining chips on the number 8 and waited. I was sweating profusely.

The croupier had his eyes fixed on me. Why was he observing me so intently? Did he suspect me of cheating? I did not really care; I just wanted the wheel to spin.

Finally, the croupier announced, "Rien ne va plus" (No more bets). My head was aching and my eyes were burning, but I managed to see the little ball land on the red 23, right next to my number 8. I looked around, searching for Eddie, hoping he would loan me some money so I could recoup my losses.

Then I saw the croupier pointing at me: "Monsieur in the blue shirt, please pick up the chips you won."

I was astonished. The croupier had set in front of me a huge number of chips of all shapes and colors, representing a small fortune, many times the amount I had started with.

I was confused and hesitant to collect the chips. Had I placed my bet on the number 23 by mistake? I was sure I had bet on the 8, but I didn't have time to think. To put an end to my hesitation, the croupier leaned toward me and whispered in Hebrew, "Avi, take them and leave. This is not a game you can win."

I picked up the chips and left the room. Who was this man, and how did he know my name? He must have attended a Jewish school in Cairo, as I had. Maybe he had seen me playing basketball with the Maccabi team.

But I didn't want to waste time on these questions. My urge to gamble had intensified with my windfall. Outside the roulette room, I met Eddie, who had lost everything he came with and had given up. He borrowed some money from me and headed to the bar, where we agreed to meet at midnight, when the casino closed.

I went to the baccarat table. I had enough chips to play respectably, despite my modest attire. I lost a good portion of my chips—albeit with dignity—and decided to go back to the roulette room.

There was a different croupier at my table. I sat down and placed a large number of chips on the number 8 again, and with every loss I bet an even larger pile of chips. I experienced all the emotions I had felt before. The same urge to try one more time, convinced that I would win.

I ended up losing all my money, and there was no one from whom I could borrow more. In any case, the croupier announced that there would be only three more spins before the casino closed.

Surprisingly, while I was heading to the bar to meet Eddie, my anxiety, my compulsions, had disappeared. In a way, I was happy to have experienced a gambler's agony for one memorable evening.

I smiled at Eddie, and he smiled back. "I lost everything," I said.

"Me, too," he replied, and we laughed. Then we joined the crowd streaming toward the casino's exit.

We got into a taxi and asked the driver to stop when the meter reached a certain amount. We wanted to have enough money left over to buy doughnuts and coffee at one of the city's many late-night cafés.

The taxi stopped in front of one such café a couple of miles away from the neighborhood where we both lived. No cup of coffee or doughnut ever tasted so good. I decided then and there never to gamble again.

During our walk home, when I told Eddie what the croupier said after I had supposedly won, he stopped and looked at me. "You lucky SOB. Basketball turned you into a celebrity. You remember that Saturday evening when we went to the movies to see Hedy Lamarr in her nude scene? The theater was full and we were ready to go home when that man offered you his tickets."

"He did it because his brother was sick," I reminded him.

"But he offered them to you instead of selling them because he was a basketball fan and he recognized you," Eddie answered.

"Yes, I remember," I said. "But that's another story!"

Gimme the Money

That Saturday morning in late December of 1956 was unusually cold. Cairo, known for its moderate winters, was not following its usual pattern. In addition, there was a fine but persistent rain falling that made the day even more gloomy.

The political situation in Cairo that year exacerbated the bleakness of the weather. President Nasser, having just prevailed over Western powers in the Suez Crisis, had proclaimed himself the leader of the Arab world. Songs praising his exploits blasted from loudspeakers all over the city. "Edbah! Edbah!" (Slaughter, slaughter) was one popular refrain directed at foreigners but mainly the Jews.

After his so-called victory, Nasser was free to purge Egypt of her enemies. He ordered the imprisonment of hundreds of Jews. He banished them from the country and confiscated their wealth and property. People emigrating from Egypt were allowed to take only their clothing and twenty Egyptian pounds—the equivalent of one hundred dollars at the time—with them. My wife, Sara, and I and our families were thinking that very soon we would also have to flee the oppressive Egyptian regime. We knew it had to happen, but we hadn't yet made a plan.

One weekend morning, I walked into the kitchen of our apartment wearing my jogging suit, hoping to find the motivation to go out for a long run, as I was accustomed to doing. I found Sara having coffee and chatting with her parents and sister, who were staying with us because their home was located on Army Street, part of a populous area of the city known as the Butchers' Quarters, where most of the riots against the Jews and foreigners began. They were talking about their situation in Egypt. Stay? Leave? And if it was best to leave, when should they go? Where should they go? How should they get there?

Sara told me, "Dad was saying that he wants to go to the bank to withdraw money in case we need it soon. But we're all against it. Going to the bank is too risky."

They were right. My father-in-law, David, had a serious heart condition, and any emotional stress could cost him his life. In addition, he would never be able to withstand the pressure of the many questions he was likely be asked by the bank's management in this hostile political climate.

That put an end to my hesitation about jogging. Going to the bank in my father-in-law's stead was the right thing to do. When I announced this to the group, they objected vehemently. I said, "You need the money, and I'm the only one here who can do it." I looked at my father-in-law and said, "Please prepare a check for me to cash while I grab my raincoat."

When I came back, I glanced at the check and was shocked by the large amount. He saw the surprise on my face. "I must start withdrawing now. There's no time to waste."

I loved Sara's father. He was quiet, methodical, and frugal. Above all, he was the most honest man I'd ever met. I slipped the check into my pocket, picked up my briefcase, kissed everyone, and left. I decided to brave the inclement weather and walk. After all, the bank was only two miles from our house.

I stopped at a nearby newspaper kiosk and greeted the proprietor, Abdel Hamid, with whom I had a good relationship. He always inquired about Sara and my in-laws. In addition to newspapers and magazines, he sold sodas and other soft drinks. But to the people he trusted, he would also sell Egypt's famous Stella beer in one-liter bottles. He did this discreetly, so as not to attract the attention of passersby. Selling alcoholic beverages on the streets was a serious offense, punishable by long prison terms.

While I was talking with Abdel, I glanced at the stack of newspapers on the bench in front of his kiosk. My eye landed on a picture of Albert Tadros on the front page of *Le Progrès Egyptien*, a French-language morning newspaper popular among people of foreign descent.

Albert Tadros was a well-known figure in Egypt. He was a high-ranking officer in the Egyptian army and the captain of two teams: the Egyptian national basketball team and the Egyptian army basketball team. Three years previously, I had played on the Maccabi team in the national championships against the Egyptian army team. I remembered Albert vividly.

The newspaper article intrigued me. I knew that Egypt had not participated in the 1956 summer Olympic Games because of the Suez Crisis. Why was Albert on the front page, then? I handed Abdel some change from the small amount of money I always carried in my jogging suit and picked up the newspaper.

Basketball was enormously popular in Egypt. It was much more than a competitive sport: it was a microcosm of all the various ethnic groups living in Egypt—the Jews, Muslims, Christians, Greeks, Italians, Armenians, and Syrians all had their own teams. But the two best teams were the Egyptian army team, representing mainly the Islamic population, and the Maccabi team, representing the Jewish population.

Unfortunately, though, the game that decided the 1953 championship did not end well. The Maccabi team won, but the Egyptian army team refused to shake our hands when the game was over, as was customary. It was the first time an opposing team had behaved that way toward us, and I was disappointed that the anti-Semitism on the streets had found its way onto the basketball court. I could no longer call Albert my friend, as I had been able to do in the past.

I opened the newspaper to the sports page and found a long article and pictures about past Olympic Games in which the Egyptian national team had participated. I was glad to see my picture in one of them, close to Zouzi Harari, our Maccabi captain and the best player on the Olympic team. I folded the newspaper with the sports page facing up and placed it in my briefcase. I intended to read the full article when I got home.

I walked nonchalantly toward the bank, reminiscing about happier days. Soon I looked up and saw that I was approaching the bank's front door.

When I took the check out of my pocket and presented it to the cashier, he looked at it for a long time. He then excused himself and walked down a long hallway behind his desk.

After a few minutes, he returned and asked me to come with him to an office in the back. He said that because the amount of the check was unusually large, he had to refer the matter to the bank manager.

I walked down the hallway with the cashier and waited in a reception area while he entered the manager's office. I picked up a *Paris Match* magazine that was lying on a table and began to leaf through it. When they called me into the manager's office, I unthinkingly took the *Paris Match* with me.

The manager was courteous but inquisitive. He asked politely to see my identification. After checking it, he asked, referring to my father-in-law, "How is Mr. Asher?"

I said, "Unfortunately, he has a very bad case of the flu. The doctor is afraid it might be pneumonia." Then I gestured at the rain-splattered window behind the manager's desk and said, "He has advised Mr. Asher to spend some time south of Egypt, in warmer and more clement weather."

The manager looked at me and said, "You know, these days the government is asking us to report any large and suspect withdrawals. But we've done business with your father-in-law for many years now, and we know he is an honest man and a good citizen." Then he asked the cashier to cash the check and bring the money back to his office.

When the cashier came back with the cash, I opened the briefcase. Then the manager handed me the *Paris Match*, which I had left on his desk. "Give it to your father-in-law; I know he'll enjoy it."

I arranged the Egyptian pounds at the bottom of my briefcase, then put the *Paris Match* on top and instinctively covered them both with the newspaper, again with the sports page facing up. When I was ready to go, the manager asked me to convey his best wishes for a speedy recovery to my father-in-law. I promised to do so, then heaved a sigh of relief as I left the bank and stepped back out onto the street.

I was happy: I had gotten the money without any problem. I was ready to go home with my mission accomplished.

After a few minutes of walking, though, I felt as if someone was following me. I passed some stores, trying to sneak a glance in the plate-glass windows, but I couldn't be sure. Then, as I turned a corner, a man caught up to me and grabbed my arm, the one that was holding the briefcase. He said he was a secret police officer and quickly whipped out his badge. He put it away again so quickly that I couldn't get a good look at it.

I released my arm forcefully and asked him what was going on. He said, "You are a spy. You have classified documents in your briefcase, and you stole money to go back to Israel."

"What?" I said in disbelief. "This is all a horrible misunderstanding."

He was trying to wrench the briefcase out of my hand. "I know you're a spy," he continued, this time in a lower tone. "I want to take you, your briefcase, your secret documents, and the money you stole to the police station so that you rot in jail. Gimme the briefcase and follow me."

"I'm not going to give you the briefcase here," I said. "I'll only give it to the officer at the police station." And I started walking with him in a most determined manner.

After a couple of minutes, he stopped and asked for the briefcase again. Once more I told him that I would give it to him only at the police station. This time I said, "I'm a basketball player and a very good friend of General Albert Tadros. I'll ask him to come to the police station; he knows who I am."

I watched as the man's face paled. He knew who Albert was, and I'm sure he believed my story. But the last thing I wanted to do was go to the police station with all that money in my briefcase. Albert would have hastened to condemn me. He hated the Maccabi players now. I had to take advantage of this man's confusion and hesitation. Besides, I couldn't argue with him any longer. I didn't want to attract the attention of passersby, who so far had not noticed us.

Audaciously, I said, "Do you want to see what's in my briefcase?" I rested it on my raised knee and opened it. The only thing visible was the sports section of the newspaper, with the picture of me and Zouzi on top. "There are no secret documents and no money—only newspapers and a magazine." I promptly closed the briefcase and added, "So if you want to, let's go to the police station, and I'll call General Tadros as soon as we get there."

I was taking a big risk with my bluff. But it was the only solution that came to mind.

I took a few steps forward, faking a resolve to go to the police station. The man did not move. "Are we going or not?" I asked.

He looked around to see if any passersby were looking at us. "All right," he whispered. "Just give me some money, and I'll let you go."

There was no way I was going to open the briefcase, and the only money I had on me was the change that remained in my jogging suit, the equivalent of thirty or forty cents. "Here," I said, handing it to him. "This the only money I have—that's the reason I'm walking home instead of taking a taxi." He took it and disappeared.

When I arrived home, everyone screamed and covered me with hugs and kisses. I wondered why their reaction was so extreme. "To what do I owe this warm reception?" I asked. I handed the briefcase to my father-in-law and sat down. He went into another room to count the money and put it away.

"Uncle Isaac came over a few minutes after you left," Sara explained, referring to my father-in-law's cousin. "He said that one of his friends and many other Jews he knew got robbed of all the money they had. They went to the bank and withdrew large amounts in preparation for their departure. Knowing what was going on, many secret police officers were waiting in front of the banks and followed them. They asked them to hand over the money under threat of being taken to the police station. They preferred to lose the money rather than end up in prison."

My father-in-law rejoined us. "Tell us—how was your visit to the bank?" he asked.

"Piece of cake," I answered.

The Ring

The two were the best friends in the whole world, closer than brother and sister. They shared everything; they trusted each other. They kept no secrets, and they said what was on their minds without filtering or holding back.

They swore their fidelity to each other during a solemn commitment ceremony held under a full moon. They held hands and mixed their blood by cutting their wrists, as they saw in a movie. They were forever bound by the pledge.

Ruby met Angel at school. She was fourteen, and Angel was twelve. He was shy and withdrawn, staying alone in a corner of the playground during recess. She was a loner, too, uninterested in the gossip and games of her classmates.

At first Ruby and Angel exchanged monosyllabic greetings. Then, gradually, as they overcame their shyness, they found common ground and shared details about their lives, their backgrounds, and their interests. They had both lost their mothers when they were little, and they both had abusive, jobless fathers who spent more time in bars than they did at home.

She was attracted to this lonely, frail boy—his pale, slim face and big blue eyes. He was attracted to this free-spirited girl, mature beyond her years. She had red hair but had dyed her braids blue. Her maverick attitude was provocative and exciting. She had tattoos all over her body and rings in her nose and lips. They were opposites irresistibly drawn to each other.

After they had been friends for a couple of months, Ruby suggested a place where they could meet out of school and away from their homes. It was a run-down shed next to an old, abandoned farmhouse a good hour's walk from town.

They lay down on the shed's floor, which was covered with straw and dried mud. Time melted away; they talked about anything that crossed their minds, sure that no one would venture close to their hideout.

Ruby lit a joint and, for the first time, allowed Angel to take a couple of tokes. He'd been asking her many times for the opportunity, but she always refused. This time, however, she agreed.

Afterward, she was worried about him and kept asking how he felt. After coughing, he said he felt happy, relaxed, and somewhat dizzy. She noticed that the joint had loosened his inhibitions; he was trying to touch her, something he had never done before.

Ruby mentioned that she had a boyfriend named Igor. He was quite a bit older than she was. "Igor is very kind and generous," she said. "He is handsome, always well dressed, and he has a nice Italian sports car. He paid for my tattoos and rings."

Angel felt betrayed. Who was this intruder? How did she meet him? Did this mean that they would not be able to get together at the shed again? He wanted to know.

Ruby had met Igor in a store. She needed to get a new shirt because the one she had was old. She had no money, so she found a store that was crowded with customers. She walked in and tried to stand near couples with children, to make it look as if she were with them.

When she found a shirt she liked, she slipped it into her bag. Unfortunately, an employee saw her and called security. As the security guard was dragging a tearful Ruby to the manager's office, they were stopped by a well-dressed man who told the guard that Ruby was with him. "He put his arm around me and said, 'Let's pay and get out of here.' That man was Igor, and he's been buying me things ever since."

"So we won't be together anymore?" Angel was ready to cry.

Ruby kissed his cheek. "What I have with Igor is not at all the same as what I have with you. You see, I like Igor because he's nice and generous. But you I love—you are more than a brother to me, and I want to be with you all the time, just as we are here, talking and laughing. You are the dearest person in my life." But Angel wanted to know more about Igor.

Even though it was early afternoon, the sky was dark, threatening rain. In the feeble light, Angel could just make out a rock pile in the corner of the shed. He wondered whether he could just bury himself in there and never come out.

"Do you have sex with him?" he asked, a lump in his throat.

Yes, she did, occasionally. "He drives us to some motels he knows, and then, if he has time, he buys me a nice dinner."

"And how often do you see him?" Like someone who's just been told he has a terminal illness, Angel wanted to find out how much time he had left.

Ruby, committed by their blood oath to hold nothing back, told the truth. "I see him maybe once or twice a week. But it's not always to have sex. He wants me to run some errands for him. I deliver packages to those mansions where the rich people live, and in turn they give me some sealed envelopes that I deliver to Igor. Sometimes he waits in his car for me."

"Do you know what the packages contain?"

Ruby didn't. She suspected they were drugs and that the envelopes were probably full of cash. "But I don't mind doing it," Ruby continued. "It makes Igor very happy. He also gives me free weed in return."

Angel didn't want to lose his time with Ruby, the only moments of happiness he had. Could they go on? He knew that Ruby was sincere when she said that she loved him.

He stood up and paced around the shed, trying to avoid the cobwebs hanging from the roof. He stood in a corner next to the rock pile. "So we can continue meeting the way we have been?"

"Absolutely," Ruby hastened to answer.

She stood up, and just as he was moving toward her, he saw a small twinkling light in a gap in the rock pile.

He knelt and slid his hand into the gap. He felt a small metal object. When he brought it out, he breathed, "It's a beautiful ring."

Ruby knelt down beside him. "Look at the size of that stone—it's huge. Do you think it's real?"

"Maybe we should take it to a jewelry store and find out," Angel suggested.

Ruby was quick to reject the idea. "It's too dangerous," she said. "They won't believe us when we tell them where we found it. They'll take us to the police, who'll ask us all kinds of questions. We can't do that."

After a moment, Ruby said, "We'd better give it to Igor. He'll know what to do. He can find out if the ring is for real without us getting in trouble."

"Are you sure?" Angel asked.

Yes, this was the best and safest solution, Ruby insisted. And by the way, she was scheduled to see Igor the following morning. She took the ring. "When you and I see each other again on Saturday, I'll have the answer for sure." She hugged him, and they left.

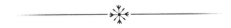

On Saturday, Angel was at the shed an hour early. When Ruby arrived—right on time—she sat on the floor and looked at him. Angel waited; he couldn't read her expression, and he did not want to rush her. Finally she said, "It's only glass."

"Are you kidding?"

"No—that is the truth. Fortunately, Igor found out without causing us any trouble."

Angel heaved a heavy sigh. "What a pity. The ring looked so lavish and expensive. It could have taken us out of our miserable lives."

Ruby stood up. "At least Igor gave me five dollars. Let's go and have ice cream."

The Store in Alexandria

When David, my father-in-law, arrived at our home in Cairo late one Friday evening for our family Shabbat dinner, we knew something was wrong.

He was livid. He had just learned that his business partner, Maurice Cohen, had been expelled from Egypt. Maurice would have to leave the country before the end of the month.

After the Suez Crisis ended with the retreat of French, British, and Israeli forces, Egypt ordered the expulsion of all citizens of those countries. Many Jews, regardless of their nationalities, were also expelled or imprisoned. Maurice and his family were Tunisians, but because Tunis was a French protectorate, they were expelled along with the French.

The expulsion of Maurice was a horrible blow to my father-in-law and consequently to our entire family.

David had inherited three retail establishments from his father—two small stores in Alexandria and one large store in Cairo. David managed the one in Cairo, and Maurice managed the two in Alexandria. Maurice was also the one who handled the accounting and administrative work related to all three stores. David took care of selling products to his longtime customers. He was not capable of running the business on his own—we all knew that.

Sara gave a glass of wine to her father and asked him to lead our kiddush prayer and Shabbat blessings. "After dinner, we can calmly discuss the matter," she said.

Our whole family had decided to immigrate to Brazil. Sara and I would go first, and my in-laws were going to follow us as soon as David had sold his stores, a task that was to be handled by Maurice. But it didn't take long to conclude that the only option we had now was for Sara and me to manage the Alexandria stores—and take care of all the other tasks Maurice used to handle—until the stores could be sold.

So Sara and I rented an apartment in Alexandria. Sara managed the smaller store, which sold women's and children's apparel as well as beach clothes, toys, and accessories, and I took care of the larger store, which sold a variety of fabrics and curtains. The store was in Souk Al Khreit, a busy street filled with shops and vendors. I also handled all matters related to David's business from an office in the store.

Our main objective was to improve the stores' performance and prepare them for sale, a mission Sara and I wanted to accomplish as soon as possible. And sure enough, it did not take long for us to reach our goals. Sara's store sold almost instantly. The owner of a nearby store bought it at our asking price.

The sale of the fabric and curtain store was more complicated. It was highly profitable and located in a very popular commercial district. We had to find the right buyer without spreading the news that the store was for sale. We didn't want to open Pandora's box by exposing David to investigation, sequestration, and even imprisonment.

I told David that he needed to find a trustworthy confidant among his Arab friends, someone who could quietly find the right purchaser, even one who was not willing or able to meet our asking price. Fortunately, finding such a trustworthy person wasn't difficult, because David maintained good relationships with many Arabs in Alexandria. The older ones had worked with his father, and the younger ones remembered seeing him when they accompanied their own fathers on business appointments.

During the days that followed, I noticed a well-dressed Arab man who came into the store, looked around, asked a few questions of our sales staff, and left. He did that a few times, then stopped. I suspected he might be a tax investigator.

Shortly thereafter, David called me on the office phone from his store in Cairo. One of his best friends in Alexandria had found the right potential buyer. "You must have seen him and maybe even talked to him; he visited the store many times last week," he said.

David and I came to a verbal agreement with the buyer. David's Arab friend was preparing the necessary documents. As soon as they were ready, David would come to Alexandria to sign them. To avoid attracting the attention of customers, employees, and the police, we decided that the closing would take place at the office of our accountant, who also served as a legal adviser. His office was only a few minutes away by car.

David came to Alexandria in the morning on the day of the closing and headed directly to the accountant's office, where his Arab friend and the buyer were expecting him. I needed to stay at the store, but David and I communicated frequently by phone to review the agreement he was about to sign. He seemed anxious and impatient during our calls. I tried to reassure him that everything was in order.

After a few minutes of silence, David called again, this time with exciting and joyful news: the documents were ready to be signed.

"Wait just a few more minutes," I said. "There's one more question I have for the accountant. Let me look up a couple of details and call you right back."

As I put down the phone, a group of six Arabs entered my office—two middle-aged men and four young men. Each of the young men was carrying a briefcase. They surrounded my desk. One of the young men got hold of the phone and kept it in his hand.

They greeted me with the traditional "As salaam alaikum" (Peace be with you). I thought surrounding my desk and taking command of my phone was a strange way to wish me peace, but I managed to stammer the usual response: "Wa alaikum as salaam wa rahmatullahi wa barakatuh" (May the peace, mercy, and blessings of Allah be upon you).

The eldest among them stepped closer to me and said that he came with his brother and their sons to buy the store. He spoke in a firm voice: "We want to buy the store now, as is, no questions asked. No documents except one page with our signatures—all in cash, now." He pointed to the briefcases the young men carried. He asked them to open them and show me that they were filled with hundred-pound notes.

I looked at the group. The two older men may have been brothers, but I doubted that the four bulky young men were their sons. They were expressionless, like four empty refrigerators, cold and huge. They almost certainly were hired guns.

I told the leader that my father-in-law was the store's owner and that he had just called me from our accountant's office to announce that he had sold the store to someone else.

The leader did not want to listen. "We already know the price he's been offered. We will pay you fifty percent more, in cash, now!"

"I'm sorry; it's over," I said.

"No, it's not over," he replied, clenching his jaw and narrowing his eyes. He then pulled up a couple of chairs, and he and his brother sat down in front of my desk. The four young men opened their jackets and, in doing so, revealed the handguns at their waists.

The young man who was holding the phone put it back in front of me. The brother, who had kept quiet until then, said calmly, "You see, we are determined to buy the store peacefully. If it's a question of price, we can discuss it and come to an agreement that will satisfy your father-in-law. Here is the phone so you can call him—but please don't call the police."

Calling the police was the last thing on my mind. We wanted to avoid giving them any indication of our departure from Egypt.

I was looking alternately at the phone and the men across from me, wondering how this would play out, when the phone rang. David and I spoke in French. He was wondering why I had asked him to wait and not sign the agreement. He said they were ready to finalize the sale and wanted to come to the store to meet with me.

I explained what was going on. I told him I could not get rid of the uninvited guests. "There are six of them, very aggressive, and they don't want to leave until we agree to sell them the store."

After a few seconds, David asked if it was a good idea for him to drive over and bring his Arab friend with him so they could put an end to the situation. "Maybe my friend can convince them that the deal is done."

"No, David," I answered. "They are armed, and it will create a disastrous confrontation." In fact, I told him I thought the men in the store *should* be the ones to buy it because they were offering 50 percent more and had the cash available in their briefcases.

David kept quiet for a second, then said, "Give me a few moments. I'll call you back."

After I hung up, the brother asked, "So what did your father-in-law say?"

I gave them a long description of David, explaining how kind and honest he was. "He really has committed to selling the store to that other buyer, and it's very difficult for him to renege on his promise."

The leader was losing his temper. "Listen—tell your father-in-law that we will double the offer. If he doesn't agree, we will kill you and burn down the store!"

I called David back to tell him about this latest development. But I didn't have a chance to do so because he immediately told me that he had explained the situation to his Arab friend and to the buyer. They both understood the seriousness of the situation and agreed to cancel the agreement.

Then I told David that I got the leader of the group to double the first buyer's offer. I could almost see David grinning from ear to ear.

"Mabrouk!" (May it be blessed) I announced to the group. "We succeeded in canceling the deal with the other buyer." The brothers grinned and shook my hand, and the four "sons" disappeared without a word, leaving the briefcases behind. The two brothers picked them up, and we took a taxi to our accountant's office, where David greeted us joyfully. After the documents were signed, the two brothers counted out the cash and left with the empty briefcases in hand.

Before catching the train back to Cairo, David came to our apartment to see Sara and celebrate the lucrative sale of the store. Sara raised a glass of wine and said, "As Avi's father used to say, 'Káthe empódio ya kaló' [Every setback is for the best]. It's amazing how this desperate situation turned out so favorably at the end."

I hugged Sara and whispered, "Now we can go to Brazil, where we can build our family and a new life."

The Hospedaria

When we arrived at the *hospedaria*—late at night, on a bus provided by HIAS, the Hebrew Immigrant Aid Society—at first I thought it was a concentration camp. There was thick barbed wire all along the high wall surrounding it, and a tower staffed with armed guards stood at one corner.

As soon as the bus pulled into the gate, the guards directed their bright tactical flashlights at us and checked our identification. Then they ordered a pair of soldiers to open the two panels of a large wooden door. We were ushered into a long hallway: on one side was a dormitory for women and children, and on the other side was a dormitory for men.

Sara, who was eight months pregnant with our first child, kissed me good night and went to the women and children's dormitory, while I went to the men's side.

The dormitory was semidark; there was just enough light for me to see my way around. There must have been more than a hundred bunk beds squeezed into a long and narrow space. My assigned bed was at the top of a bunk tucked away in a corner.

This was our introduction to Brazil. We had gotten off a ship mere hours earlier after more than two weeks at sea, and then were bused here to São Paulo with little more than the clothes on our backs. We didn't know the language, and I had no prospects for employment.

Early the following morning, I found Sara waiting on a bench in the hallway. Judging by her pale face and the dark circles under her eyes, I knew she hadn't slept. When I asked her what happened, she said, "Imagine hell, then think worse!" Half-naked women were fighting over beds. They did not bother to use the facilities. Sara had been assigned a bottom bunk that she didn't sleep in because it was covered with urine and feces that had dropped down from the top bunk.

I had to get Sara out of this awful situation. But how?

As I was in the hallway comforting Sara, I saw Moti, my childhood friend, rushing toward us with open arms, ready to give us a good, warm *abraço*—a traditional Brazilian hug. He had heard from another Egyptian immigrant that Sara and I had arrived and hurried over to the *hospedaria* to find us. As soon as he saw Sara, he told us that she should stay with him in the small home he shared with his wife and young son until I found work. Sara and I gratefully accepted his generous offer. Relieved that she was in a safe place, I could get my documents in order, find a job, and earn enough money to rent a small apartment for Sara, myself, and the baby.

But to do all that, I had to stay at the *hospedaria* for a few more weeks.

On my third day, braving the shower facilities, where I stood in filthy water up to my knees, I bathed as best as I could. Then I put on my only presentable suit and headed to Rua Quinze de Novembro, a one-mile-long street where the city's banks were headquartered.

I knocked on the doors of all the banks on both sides of the street. My visits followed a pattern: a concierge would answer the door and introduce me to a human resources officer who would offer me a cafezinho, a small cup of strong sweetened coffee. I would explain my situation in the few

Portuguese words I knew, augmented by plenty of French and hand gestures. The answers were almost identical: "Unfortunately, we have no vacancy at the moment. Good luck in your search."

After spending many anxious hours methodically knocking on doors and being turned down just as methodically, I stopped at the end of the street to catch my breath. It was past four in the afternoon. Very soon the bank doors would be closing for the day. It was winter in São Paulo, but I was sweating from anxiety, and my stomach was churning from the many cafezinhos I had drunk—and from the sadness and apprehension I felt about the future.

The only building remaining was the large and imposing Banco do Estado, the state bank, which I was told would never hire recent immigrants. But after I walked a few steps farther, I saw a small building that was almost hidden by the imposing state bank. After a few more steps, I realized that it was another bank, the Banco Brasul de São Paulo.

I was tired and discouraged, wondering whether it was even worth trying one more time. But I wiped my face, brushed off my jacket, and knocked on the door.

An old man with white hair opened it. Like the concierges at the other banks, he offered me a chair in the reception room. After repeating the same story I'd told at the other banks, I was surprised to see that this man really was interested. He asked many questions about my background, about my family, and about Egypt.

I asked him whether he thought the bank would hire me—an immigrant with no knowledge of Portuguese and no previous banking experience. I didn't have much to offer, but I needed the job badly.

The man offered me a glass of cold water and said that the vice president of human resources was in a meeting in the conference room at that moment. He said he would take me to meet her.

We took the elevator up to the second floor and stopped in front of a large door. I felt like my whole life depended on what was behind it.

Fifteen or more men and women were seated around a long oval table. The person running the meeting was a middled-aged woman who I guessed was the human resources vice president.

As soon as we entered, she stood up, and the whole group stood up with her. The old man put his hand on my shoulder and said, "This is Avi. He arrived here as an immigrant from Egypt less than three days ago. He doesn't speak our language, but he managed to sustain a conversation with me for almost an hour. He is a good man. I want you to find him a job and hire him today." Then he shook my hand and left.

The vice president showed me to her office and offered me a job in the exchange department, where my French would be useful. I thanked her profusely. But all the time I kept thinking of the old man, and finally I asked about him. She said he was one of the bank's owners. "He is a very kind man," she said.

A kind man? I thought. He is an angel!

I went to Moti's home the next day to tell Sara the good news. She didn't stop kissing me and hugging me. We opened the bottle of brandy I had won on the ship in a table tennis contest and celebrated my new job. "Now I can have our baby!" Sara said, her face aglow.

While working at the bank, I continued to stay at the *hospedaria* because we hadn't yet saved enough money to live on our own. The *hospedaria* provided me with breakfast, dinner, and a place to sleep. In addition, as long as I was there, I could count on HIAS for assistance with my paperwork and immigration status. The world looked brighter from all angles.

I quickly adjusted to life at the *hospedaria*. I woke up before five in the morning to take a shower—if I took it any later, the floor would be flooded—then got dressed, ate breakfast, and went to work. With less anxiety, I slept better. My top bunk in the men's dormitory became more comfortable, and that provided me the rest I needed to handle my job.

The dormitory was full of men of many races and religions. In addition to the immigrants from various countries, the *hospedaria* also housed a large contingent of poor Brazilians from the northwest part of the country fleeing drought and hunger and hoping to find work in São Paulo. Some of these men and others gathered on the bunk bed beneath mine. They sometimes lit candles and played cards late at night, gambling while everyone else was asleep. The organizer of these games was a big, heavy man who bunked below me. I guessed he was from Eastern Europe. We never spoke. He didn't bother me, and I didn't bother him.

One night I went to bed early, as was my habit, expecting another restful and uneventful night. I was fast asleep when I suddenly was awakened by a cacophony of loud voices. I opened my eyes and saw a group of policemen barking orders, shining their flashlights over the bunks. I could see that one of the gamblers was lying on the floor in a pool of blood. Others had been handcuffed and were standing against the wall.

The police were pointing their guns at the big, heavy man who slept under me. He was leaning against my bed and held a bloodstained knife in his hand.

He was yelling in a language I could not understand. When the policemen came closer, the heavy man jumped on my bed with astonishing agility. He sat behind me and pulled me against him. He had one arm around my throat while the other held the knife over my chest.

In broken Portuguese, he asked the policemen to leave the *hospedaria* and send him money and a car within the hour. He would hold me hostage until all his requests were fulfilled.

At first I couldn't believe the scene that was unfolding before my eyes. Was I in a movie? Was I dreaming?

Then I panicked. What would happen if the police didn't give him everything he asked for? And even if they did, where would I end up?

There was a long moment of silence during which I did the only thing I could do—beg the man to let me go. Instead, he pressed the knife against my cheek, hard enough to break the skin. A few drops of blood fell to my chest. He wanted to show that he meant business.

The policemen must have asked for reinforcements, because what seemed to be a SWAT team joined them. This was not good news for me: it meant they were getting ready to confront my captor.

I could feel the big, heavy man getting extremely nervous. His body was shaking. Every time he moved, the bed would squeak, and that added more anxiety to the already scary situation.

Was this the end of all my dreams? I wouldn't be able to see Sara and our baby. All the work and pain we had gone through to come to Brazil and build a new life was about to end in this senseless confrontation.

I'm not religious; I lost any faith I had when my mother died, a week before my tenth birthday. But at that moment in the *hospedaria*—I don't know why—I recited the Shema, just as I and my childhood friends had done instinctively every time we were scared or in a difficult situation.

Suddenly, with a loud cracking sound, the bunk sagged. The big, heavy attacker rolled off the side and fell on his head. I fell off the other side, landing on my back, and the knife went rolling away from us.

It didn't take but a second for the police to rush over, handcuff the attacker, and take him away. I was safe.

When I told the story to Sara, she said, "It's your mother who watches over you." She added, "Now you can have faith again: the Shema helped you, too."

Carlos's Wedding

I

I met Carlos when I was working at the Brazilian subsidiary of the multinational company where I had been employed for a number of years. I had just been promoted to sales manager, and Carlos—whose family was originally from Spain but whose father had been born in Ohio, where Carlos had been living—was the person appointed to fill my previous position. Everyone liked him for his work ethic, his energy, his enthusiasm, and, above all, his affable personality.

Carlos and I became friends. He would come to our home, eat dinner with us, help Sara in the kitchen, play with the children, and even read them stories when it was time for them to go to bed.

One evening after dinner, he announced to Sara and me that he was very much in love with a woman he had met at a party.

"What's her name?" Sara asked.

"Juracy," Carlos answered, a dreamy, faraway look in his eyes.

Juracy was the daughter of a well-established Brazilian family. Her mother was a pharmacist and her father a famous doctor. She worked as an assistant to the president of a huge automobile corporation. Carlos was madly in love with her.

"She's the woman I want to spend the rest of my life with," he said.

But after two years in Brazil and proving how skillful and efficient he was at his job, Carlos was promoted to sales manager of the company's subsidiary in Colombia, a promotion he couldn't turn down.

Before he left Brazil, he came to our house to announce his transfer. "So we won't see you anymore?" Sara lamented.

I said, "Don't worry: Carlos has one big reason to come here at every opportunity!"

He smiled. Yes, he had promised Juracy that he'd spend holidays with her in São Paulo. In addition, he told Sara that he was going to ask Juracy to marry him. He planned to ask for her parents' blessing on his next trip to São Paulo. He wanted me to be present.

"Why?" Sara asked.

"Because I want Avi to be my best man."

Sara and I looked at each other, surprised.

Sara hugged him and said, "Carlos, you're the third person from the company to ask Avi to be his best man. What a popular husband I have!"

"It's not that I'm popular," I rejoined. "It's because no one else would do it!" They both laughed.

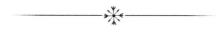

On the Saturday when Carlos planned to ask Juracy for her hand, the plan was for us to have breakfast with our family at home, then I would drive him to Juracy's parents' house.

Carlos and I left midmorning. We got in my company car, a black Cadillac—a fringe benefit that had come with my promotion. Carlos had written down the directions on a business card Juracy had given him, so we were confident we could find our way.

During the journey, we updated each other about our work and colleagues. We also talked about recent political events. I told him that after the military coup that had just taken place in Brazil, the new government, appointed by Marshal Humberto de Alencar Castelo Branco, had outlawed all opposing political parties and imposed draconian measures to control prices, increase taxes, and restrict monetary transfers out of the country.

Brazilians were hostile toward their new leaders. Rumors circulated that politicians, university students, and artists were being tortured and killed. Many of them had disappeared.

As we entered an unfamiliar part of the city, the streets got much narrower. I wanted to be careful not to hit any parked cars or pedestrians who carelessly made their way between them. I had just turned my head to ask Carlos whether we were headed in the right direction when suddenly a military truck sped in front of us then abruptly stopped, blocking our way.

Six soldiers jumped off the truck and saluted a highly decorated officer who was walking toward us. He had what looked like dozens of stars on his uniform. The soldiers were carrying machine guns, and the officer carried a .44 Magnum in his hand. The soldiers stood at attention by his side and yelled, "Yes, General," anytime he breathed so much as a single word.

The general wanted us to open the doors of the Cadillac, which Carlos and I had locked as soon as the scene began to unfold. I lowered my window just enough to be able to communicate with him.

"You two foreigners are under arrest!" he barked. The soldiers immediately pointed their machine guns at us, ready to shoot.

I calmly asked the reason for our arrest. He answered that we were spies and that he planned to take us to a place where the authorities could check our identification and interrogate us. He wanted us to leave the car and get in his truck.

By that time a few more soldiers had surrounded the car, and some passersby had stopped to watch. I hoped their presence would prevent the soldiers from using their guns. However, no one dared interfere with the general.

I told the general that we were not spies and that the whole thing was a big misunderstanding. Maybe he had mistaken us for someone else? The general did not want to hear it; he ordered us out of the car.

Finally, in a firm voice, I told him, "General, we will not leave the car. If you want to, go ahead and shoot us. But we will stay in the car."

He was perplexed, clearly not knowing what to do. Given his two options—let us go or shoot us—there was no chance he would let us go, not in front of his soldiers and not after all his bluster.

Worried about the fact that he was cornered and left only with the shooting option, I quickly proposed that we follow his truck to the closest police station. That, I said, should satisfy his need to bring us before the authorities.

Reluctantly, he agreed.

We followed the truck to a dark gray three-story building with large brown double doors in front. One of the soldiers got out of the truck, ran to the door, and said or did something that caused it to open slowly, allowing the truck and our car to drive through.

One soldier and one police officer, each holding a machine gun, were standing on either side of the door. We were in a large courtyard covered by a dirty, muddy glass roof.

Carlos whispered, "What kind of police station is this—in a decrepit building, with no identification in front, staffed with military *and* police officers?"

I told him I didn't know but that we needed to be calm. We didn't have any other choice.

After we waited for what seemed like an eternity, more soldiers appeared out of nowhere and stood behind our car. Then they ordered us to follow the truck, which was driving down a narrow alley at the end of the courtyard.

When the truck stopped, the soldiers ordered us to get out of the car. They searched us and took our wallets, watches, rings, and money, except for a few large bills I had placed in a hidden pocket in my slacks.

The general and his crew got out of their truck. They opened the door to another building, and we all entered what seemed to be a theater with many empty chairs. We were ordered to sit in the center of the front row, facing a long table placed on a platform. A row of chairs stood behind the table.

The general left and came back accompanied by six men, five of whom were wearing black robes and black masks. The sixth man, who seemed to be the leader, wore a white robe and a white mask. They sat down on the chairs behind the table, the leader in white in the center and the general at his right.

The leader spoke slowly, making sure he clearly articulated every syllable. His voice was saccharine but solemn.

"The general brought you here because you are spies, a capital offense that calls for the death penalty."

I was holding Carlos's hand because he was shaking.

"This panel of military judges will render its verdict in the morning. Meanwhile, you'll be locked in a secure cell."

I could not restrain Carlos, who jumped out of his chair. Pointing his finger at the judges, he screamed, "You are all crazy! What is this travesty?" When he saw several soldiers rushing toward him, he shouted at the top of his lungs, "I want to call the American embassy!" But the soldiers were all over him. They forced his hands behind his back and handcuffed him.

II

The cell they locked us in was so dark that we could hardly see each other. Amazingly, despite the life-and-death situation, Carlos had become very calm and still. He asked me, "Okay, here we are in this crazy place with crazy people who could easily kill us tomorrow. How are we going to get out of here?"

I told him that what we were going through reminded me of Kafka's *The Trial*.

"Who's Kafka?" Carlos asked.

"He's a writer of some weird stories. In *The Trial*, the main character ends up being found guilty and executed with a double-edged butcher knife."

"Very reassuring," Carlos muttered.

What to do? I knew that Carlos was counting on me to find a way out. I felt guilty for leading us both to this place, although I had been following the directions he had dictated to me from the card he held in the car.

We were both quiet for a while. Then a surge of hope went through me.

"Carlos, what was that card you were holding when you were reading me the directions to Juracy's parents' house?"

"Nothing important. It's Juracy's father's business card; I scribbled the address and the directions on the back. I think it's still in my shirt pocket."

"Come closer; let me see if you still have it." I fished the card out of his breast pocket, but of course I couldn't read it in the dark. "Do you think their home phone number is on the card?"

Yes; Carlos remembered seeing it. "How is that going to help us?" He sounded desperate.

It was an extremely long shot, like winning the lottery, but I told Carlos it was worth a try. My mother used to say, "Tant qu'il y a la vie, il y a l'espoir" (As long as there is life, there is hope).

Through the gloom, I could just make out a soldier sitting on a chair and smoking a cigarette in the distance. I called to him: "Senhor, senhor, por favor venha aqui" (Sir, sir, please come here). After I begged him many times in this fashion, he finally brought his chair over and sat close to our cell, making sure, however, to leave his gun out of our reach.

When I asked him about the place we were in, he said that many people—young and old, men and women—had passed through it, having been brought here the same way we were. Most of them disappeared afterward. He did not know where or how. It seemed to me he was just relieved to find someone to talk to.

Then I asked many questions about him, his family, and his job. His name was Pedro. He was married and had five children, and this was his second year in the army. His monthly salary was probably not even a third of what I had in my hidden pocket. And, he said cheerfully, he was going home in less than an hour. Another soldier would take his place and guard us the rest of the night.

I brought my face close to the iron bars that separated us. "Do you want to make three times more money tonight than you make in a month?" I asked.

He moved his chair backward.

"No, I'm not asking you to let us out of the cell. It's too dangerous for you, and there is no way we can get out of this building. What I'm asking is that you call a doctor we know. Just tell him we are in prison and give him the address of this building." I had the money in my hand and extended it through the bars to him.

He hesitated for a second, then grabbed the money.

"You promise?" I asked.

"Yes, I promise," he whispered, then shook my hand.

Carlos was suspicious. "That soldier will take your money and maybe even report you to his superiors. This will not help. You're too naive and trusting." I didn't blame him for being pessimistic. After all, he was probably right. But what else could we do?

The soldier who replaced Pedro was from Ceará, a state in the northeastern part of the country that was also home to Marshal Castelo Branco. We asked for food and water, but he refused. "Tomorrow they'll interrogate you again, and if you don't tell them everything they want to know, they will blindfold you, stand you up against the wall in the courtyard, and shoot you," he said. I could almost see the sadistic smile on his face.

Carlos and I sat on the cell's cement floor. The only thing we could do was wait. Maybe Pedro would keep his promise.

Sometime later, we fell asleep. At one point, Carlos woke up from a nightmare, mumbled something incoherent, then went back to sleep. Just after I nodded off again, I woke up and saw him grabbing the iron bars of the cell and yelling, "Who are you?" He was holding the bars as if he were trying to break them in two.

Fortunately, someone had turned the lights on. I could see a group of people approaching us—three army officers and a civilian. They were followed by the general and the judge in the white robe. But this time, the judge was without his mask.

The cruel soldier who had been guarding us opened the cell and politely let us out. The civilian was Juracy's father. He was the chief doctor of the Brazilian army. After he received the call from Pedro, he had called the highest-ranking officers in the military and asked them for help. They came to our cell after meeting with the judges and the general—who, Juracy's father told us, was actually a colonel and was under the influence of drugs and alcohol.

The colonel approached us, humble, subdued, and apologetic. He was now the fearful one—fearful that we would file charges against him. "Please forgive me. I made a big mistake; what can I do to make it right?" he asked.

"You can go to hell," Carlos replied.

Our entire family went to Carlos and Juracy's wedding. He was radiant, and she was gorgeous in her satin wedding gown.

At the reception, I raised my glass of Champagne and proposed a toast: "As the only best man in history who went to jail for the groom, I want to wish you both a long, prosperous, and happy life together."

Sara had tears streaming down her cheeks, both relieved that my nightmarish adventure was over and joyful that our dear friend Carlos was marrying Juracy, the love of his life.

She and I danced to Jacques Brel's song "Ne me quitte pas."

"Don't you ever leave me," she whispered in my ear.

The Madman (O Trelós)

*H*e lived in a small mountainous village in northern Greece, probably one of the poorest villages in the country.

It had only one grocery store, which sold small quantities of a bit of everything. Food and beverages could be found alongside toys, pens, paperback books, and small housewares.

The village had one antique fire truck that doubled as an ambulance. An old school bus took passengers twice a day to a larger village around an hour away.

Two-thirds of the village residents were Christian; the other third were Muslim. The population of five hundred was in steady decline. The village was unable to stop the exodus of young people who preferred to try their luck in places with better economic conditions.

The man lived alone in a house with a small backyard. It was built by his father, who completed it just a few days before he married a beautiful Albanian woman, a member of a very religious Muslim family. Her father and older brothers were furious when she fell in love with a Christian and threatened to kill her for the offense. Nevertheless, the wedding took place under the protection of the Greek community.

The couple wanted to have a child, but they weren't able to conceive for a couple of decades. At last they succeeded, but the delivery was painful, and it almost cost the mother her life. When the baby was born, they were overjoyed to discover that it was the boy they had been praying for. They named him Dionysos, after the Greek god of wine, fruit, fertility, and ritual madness—the god of life, enjoyment, fun, and a carefree spirit.

Their joy, however, lasted only a couple of years. It turned into sadness when they discovered that their son did not meet the developmental milestones expected of a two-year-old. They took him to the neighboring town and had him examined by a doctor, who diagnosed severe delays in motor and language skills. He told the parents that their boy was mentally impaired.

Dionysos could not attend school, but he developed great physical prowess. He could outrun any other boy his age. He was also an adept hiker and swimmer. He could talk in short sentences but had a pronounced stutter that, over time, people gradually came to understand.

When Dionysos was twenty years old, his parents were killed in a horrible accident. The old school bus they were riding in, carrying them to the nearby town, careened over one of the village's steep hillsides and crashed into the ravine below. Many other people traveling with Dionysos's parents were also killed. The accident affected numerous families in the village, Christian and Muslim.

Dionysos refused to go to an institution or leave the village. He knew all the people there, and they all knew him. By that time, they did not refer to him by name: they called him O Trelós, the crazy man. He lived off the money they gave him and off the food, drinks, and other products the owner of the grocery store offered him. Many times, he paid the villagers back by running errands for them. Sometimes he would do or say something odd, but people did not mind. As a matter of fact, they loved him.

While he was still a relatively young man, though, his behavior became even more odd. He started knocking on doors in the afternoons and early evenings, muttering about some lost pet or object. Still, people preferred to ignore such interruptions, attributing them to Dionysos's mental illness.

But things got worse. Dionysos began knocking on doors in the wee hours, screaming that a ghost with a knife was trying to get into his bedroom. He saw the apparition at the window, lurking in the darkness. The villagers reached the point where they did not open the door for him anymore.

The strategy worked, because for a long time after that, O Trelós did not bother them.

Early one morning, one of the village elders stopped by Dionysos's house to see what had happened to the crazy man. He knocked on the door. Not getting an answer, he went to the alley behind the house and looked through window into Dionysos's bedroom.

He saw Dionysos lying on his bed, but he couldn't tell whether he was sleeping or if there was a problem. So he summoned the neighbors, and they forced the front door open. When they got to the bedroom, they found Dionysos on his back, dried blood covering the sheets. His throat had been slit from one side to the other.

The village went into mourning. They realized that Dionysos was not as crazy as they had thought; someone—or something—really had been after him.

The authorities wanted to find out who could have committed such despicable act, but the police force was tiny and didn't have the manpower or means to investigate. So they classified the murder as a cold case. Rumor had it that Dionysos's mother's Muslim family was responsible, but no one pursued this possibility.

One night around a year later, a young couple saw a shadow at their bedroom window. Judging by its shape, they thought it looked like a man holding a knife. They noticed the shadow again the following night and for two or three nights after that, always at the same time. The couple was so concerned that they talked to their neighbors, and they decided to set a trap.

The next night, fifteen minutes before the shadow usually appeared, a group of five neighbors hid behind the bushes at one side of the window. Another group of neighbors hid behind the bushes on the opposite side.

Finally, a disheveled middle-aged man with long hair and a long beard showed up, holding a knife in his hand. They caught him! As it turned out, he was not from the village but rather was a vagrant who wandered from mountain hamlet to mountain hamlet, terrorizing the residents wherever he went. People had seen him staggering in the street or sitting on the sidewalk, a bottle of ouzo in his hand.

It didn't take long for this man to confess. He was the one who killed O Trelós. He had also attacked people in other small towns.

The villagers unanimously decided to name the street in front of Dionysos's house Odós Trelós (Madman Street).

The Tonsillectomy

That Friday night, I was in Fortaleza, a beautiful city in northeastern Brazil. I was tired but happy. As the sales manager for my company's Brazilian subsidiary, I had finally succeeded in persuading our biggest customer to sign a major new contract with us. We had just sealed our agreement with a handshake over dinner.

It was late when I retired to my hotel room, too late to call Sara in São Paulo. I would call her the next morning. I went to bed and turned out the lights, ready to sleep, when the phone rang. It was Sara: everything was fine except for our younger daughter Hanna, four years old at the time.

"As you know, she hasn't been feeling well these last few weeks. But now she's in real pain. She has a fever, and her ears and throat hurt. I took her to the pediatrician this morning. He recommended that we take her to a doctor he knows, a professor of pediatrics who practices at the

Albert Einstein Hospital. He sent a message to the professor, whose office called me this afternoon; he can see us Monday morning. Can you be back this weekend?"

"Yes, I'll be home," I replied immediately.

I still had some work to do the following week, but I had already accomplished the chief goal of my trip. I could postpone my visits to the company's other customers without a problem. They would understand the situation.

Midmorning on Monday, Sara, Hanna, and I went to see the professor at the hospital, which was known as one of the best medical facilities in Brazil, if not the world. Soon after our arrival, a nurse called us in, and we followed her to the professor's office.

He stood up from behind his desk and came toward us with a smile. He shook hands with Sara and me and took Hanna in his arms. "What's wrong with you, beautiful Hanna?" he cooed.

After listening to Sara's description of Hanna's symptoms, he put her down and examined her throat and ears. Her throat was infected, and so were her ears, as a result of her swollen and infected tonsils.

Using what sounded to me like a practiced version of baby talk, he told her, "When Daddy and Mommy bring you back here, I'll take these ugly things out of your mouth, and you won't have any owies anymore." Then, whispering in her ear, he added, "You will also get my special ice cream!"

He prescribed an antibiotic for the infection and scheduled the surgery for a date two weeks away—a Wednesday, a day I could take off from work.

Hanna did not seem impressed by the professor. Judging by the expression on her face, I guessed she wasn't taken in by his syrupy tone. Mention of the ice cream didn't seem to make a difference, either.

But Sara and I thought he was a nice, respectful man. He was in his late fifties or early sixties and had a dignified and graceful allure, that of an experienced practitioner who was confident in his skills.

While we were thanking him, he looked at his watch and told us he had to hurry and join members of the hospital's senior management team for lunch. Sara and I apologized for the delay we caused, but he waved our apology off and explained, "Don't worry. The conference room is just here in front of my office, and the hospital's cafeteria brings our lunch. It happens every Monday."

On the Wednesday of the surgery, Sara, Hanna, and I went to the professor's office. He greeted us with the same self-confidence he had demonstrated during our first visit. Hanna was amazingly quiet and calm while the nurse prepared her for the operation. Meanwhile, the professor reassured us that he had performed thousands of successful tonsillectomies with zero complications. All perfect.

He said the procedure would take less than an hour, and then we could see Hanna in the recovery room. "You'll be home in two to three hours, max."

And indeed, in less than an hour, we were told that Hanna was in the recovery room. We went in and waited until she opened her eyes. She did not talk but gave us to understand that she wanted to go home.

Once we were back at our house and settled in, Sara mentioned that it might be a good idea to bring Hanna's bed into our bedroom in case she needed something in the middle of the night. Yes, I agreed; it was a good idea.

At bedtime, Hanna did not want to talk; she just wanted to lie down in her bed. Sara tried to give her a dose of the medicine the professor prescribed to alleviate her pain and help her sleep, but Hanna didn't want any of it. She just wanted to sleep.

Sara and I then spent some time in the living room, sipping glasses of wine, happy that the surgery went well. Then we went to our bedroom and fell asleep.

Sara did not know why she woke up in the middle of the night. She thought maybe she heard heavy breathing. She turned the light on and went to check on Hanna. As soon as she got to the bed, though, Sara gave out a terrifying yell: "Avi, come quick!" I jumped out of bed and joined her. Hanna's face was blue, her mouth wide open. She was gasping for air.

I took Hanna in my arms. I had no idea what to do at that late hour. There was no way I could have gotten her to a hospital in time. All that went through my mind in a fraction of a second.

I instinctively grabbed Hanna's feet and held her upside down in the air. She was suffocating. I shook her and gave her a firm rap on her back. Then she cried loudly and coughed up a large piece of cotton gauze full of blood. The professor and his staff had evidently left it in her throat.

When Hanna finally stopped crying, we watched her breathe normally for a while, then let her go back to sleep.

Sara and I stayed awake the rest of the night, happy to have saved Hanna but at the same time angry with our self-confident, dignified professor.

The next morning, I placed the bloody gauze in a box and put it in my briefcase. Intrigued, Sara asked, "Are you showing it to your colleagues at work?"

"I'm not sure; maybe," I replied.

After a week had passed, Hanna was recovering nicely. But I was still upset and angry—no, that wasn't it. I was disappointed. Doctors must not err, especially when it comes to their postsurgical checklists. It's as simple as that. Just as airline pilots do before takeoff, they must go through an exacting routine with built-in redundancy. There must be zero risk of a mistake.

At the office, I wrote my thoughts down on a piece of paper to help me calm down. It was lunchtime, so I slipped the paper in my briefcase and left the office.

While I was walking to a restaurant where I often met some of my colleagues, I realized that I was just a few minutes away from the hospital where Hanna had her operation. It's Monday, I thought. The professor must be with his senior management team in the conference room. I'm going to pay him a visit.

I opened the door to the conference room and saw the professor seated at the far end of a long table, his lunch in front of him. He had probably just told a joke; the other people in the room were laughing with him.

Caught by surprise, the whole group was staring at me as I walked toward the professor. "Please don't worry," I told them. "I'm just dropping something off."

I opened my briefcase, took the lid off the box, and placed the bloody gauze on the professor's rib-eye steak. "Professor, this belongs to you. You left it in the throat of my four-year-old daughter, who almost suffocated last week. And this is a note from her father." I threw the note on his lap and left.

That night, I felt good. Hanna was cheerful, and Sara wore her sweet, charming smile.

"What did you ever do with the box you took with you last week?" she asked.

"I put it back where it belongs."

A Trip to Remember

*Y*amin Baruch was standing in the doorway of his house in Paris, his briefcase and overnight bag lying on the welcome mat. He had just hugged his wife goodbye; now it was time to hop in his Renault 4CV for a business trip to the South of France.

At thirty-two, Yamin was the youngest PDG (président-directeur général) in France and probably in all of Europe. A PDG in France holds a higher position than that of a chief executive officer in the United States. And Yamin was the PDG of a very large company, which carried an even greater degree of prestige.

Each spring, he visited the company's regional offices and major accounts on his own, without any of his associates. He did not want to be influenced by his subordinates. He wanted to see and hear his district managers, employees, and key customers without any filter or interference. He wanted to form his own opinion firsthand.

And instead of taking his chauffeur-driven limousine for these trips, he liked to drive his own 4CV, a car his wife had driven for a long time and passed on to him when she got a new one. Yamin wanted to show modesty in the presence of the people he met, especially when holding meetings with workers and union leaders.

Yamin had been recruited to turn around the operations of his company, which had been losing a lot of money for several years. But after only eighteen months on the job, he had succeeded in converting the company's heavy losses into substantial profits and laying the groundwork for sustainable results in the future.

On this trip, Yamin's first stop was Marseille, home to the most important operation in the southern region. He spent a few days reviewing business matters with the district manager, talking with the employees, and visiting customers. He also visited the Nice operation and the customers in the surrounding areas.

On his way back, he planned to visit Lyon, where the company maintained a smaller operation. After that, he would drive directly home and arrive in time for the Friday Shabbat dinner, as he'd promised his wife.

To get to Lyon, he left early in the morning and took the A6, also known as the Autoroute du Soleil (motorway of the sun). Yamin felt calm and happy, enjoying the beautiful weather and admiring the sunrise, which created a faint rainbow in the deep blue sky. He arrived at the Lyon office just after 1:00 p.m., greeted the receptionist, and glanced at the morning newspaper lying on a table. At the bottom of the first page, he spotted a headline: ENCORE TROIS SUICIDES (Three more suicides).

The receptionist explained that there had been a wave of suicides among the youth in Lyon, "mainly teenage girls, victims of bullying at their schools." She added that the media was pressing the schools' principals and local authorities to take action to stop the bullying.

"I hope those efforts bear fruit," Yamin said.

Just then the district manager came out of his office and shook Yamin's hand. They headed to the conference room where their meeting was to take place. Just outside the room, a man was seated on a chair. When he saw Yamin and the district manager, he stood up. The district manager went to him and whispered a few words; the man went back to his seat.

When they entered the conference room and closed the door behind them, the district manager explained that the man was Alain, one of his best salesmen. Unfortunately, he had to fire Alain because he was an alcoholic and created many problems with customers and colleagues. Also, he was absent half the time. The company had tried every means at its disposal to help him, all to no avail. "He's waiting outside because he heard you were coming and wants to talk to you," the district manager said.

The Lyon district was very well run, and there were not many issues to discuss. After around an hour, the district manager asked permission to invite Alain into the room.

When Alain came in, he apologized and spoke with poise. He said he understood the reasons why he was fired. He recognized that the company had done all it could to help him and admitted that he was the one to be blamed.

"Monsieur Baruch, when I heard you were visiting today, I wanted to see you and thank you for all the good years I spent with this company."

Yamin shook his hand and begged him to take care of his health.

Alain then said, "There is another reason I'm here. I know how keen you are to keep abreast of our competitors' activities. There is a new product our major competitor is testing secretly at the shop of one of my important customers. This customer also happens to be my friend and is willing to show it to you today if you can come with me."

Yamin was of course interested, but he asked Alain to wait another half hour or so because he was about to meet with all the employees and brief them on the state of the company.

When he was ready, Yamin put his briefcase in his 4CV's trunk and got into Alain's car. After a few minutes, Alain turned onto a hilly thoroughfare that led to the mountains and a ski resort.

Yamin asked him whether his customer was located very far from the Lyon office. Instead of answering, Alain pressed the accelerator to the floor.

The car started shuddering and swerving from side to side on the narrow, winding two-way road. Yamin was alarmed and ordered Alain to slow down.

"Monsieur Baruch, I'm not the only one who lost his job today. You'll be losing yours, too, together with your life. I'm going to crash the car into a boulder and kill us both, or I'm going to find a high cliff and drive the car off the precipice. Which do you prefer?"

Yamin was shocked by Alain's sudden metamorphosis. The calm and poised man he met at the office had just turned into a suicidal murderer. The car was screeching around each curve, barely missing the steep drop-offs. Miraculously, there was no oncoming traffic.

Yamin tried appealing to reason. "Why don't we get off at the next exit and talk this through? There are plenty of people who want to help you—you won't have to go it alone."

Alain kept his eyes straight ahead. The tires squealed around a sharp bend as he sawed the steering wheel back and forth. The engine gave off a terrifying roar, and Yamin thought he could smell smoke.

Finally, on one of the sharpest double curves, Alain lost control. The car skidded into a grass-covered ditch and stopped just short of a tree.

Yamin heaved a sigh of relief. The crazy ride was over. But when he turned to look at Alain, he came face-to-face with the barrel of a gun, which Alain was pointing unsteadily at Yamin's head.

"Monsieur Baruch, it's time to say goodbye." He locked all the doors from the controls on his armrest. "First I'm going to kill you, then I'm going to kill myself."

There was no doubt that Alain was perfectly serious. Yamin visualized the newspaper headline the Lyon receptionist would have on the table the next morning: ET MAINTENANT IL Y EN A QUATRE (And now there are four).

Yamin spoke in a low and quiet voice. He asked Alain whether he had a wife and children.

Alain nodded but kept the gun pointed at Yamin's head.

"Alain, you're young," Yamin said. "You have a family waiting for you. What will happen to them if you don't show up tonight?"

A timid knock on the driver's-side window interrupted Yamin's plea.

Alain tucked the gun between his legs and lowered his window. A little girl, around four or five years old, was holding out a bunch of brightly colored wildflowers. "I picked these myself. I gave a bouquet to my mom, but I wanted to give one to you and your friend because you both look so sad."

The girl had wide blue eyes and an open, freckled face. Alain gently took the wildflowers from her hand.

The girl smiled, then turned around and went running back to her mother, who was standing by her car watching.

Alain whispered, "She looks like Annie, my youngest daughter!" He tossed the flowers on the back seat, threw the gun on Yamin's lap, and then lowered his head onto the steering wheel and sobbed loudly.

Yamin put a comforting hand on Alain's shoulder. "Alain, you have a whole happy life ahead of you. Don't waste it." He reached out and took the car keys and slipped them and the gun into his jacket pocket. Alain was no longer dangerous.

As Yamin drove the car out of the ditch, he and Alain waved to the girl, who was looking at them from the back seat of her mother's car.

By the time they arrived at the Lyon office parking lot, everyone had left for the day. Assuming a serious tone, Yamin told Alain that he would not report the incident to the authorities provided that he seek treatment for his debilitating addiction. Then he handed Alain his car keys and got in the 4CV.

When he arrived home late that evening, his wife was waiting for him. "Why are you so late? Any problems?"

"No," Yamin hastened to say. "Just traffic issues."

"Shabbat shalom," she replied. "Let's say the kiddush blessings."

Chania

I

Here's an interesting story about something that happened during one of our family vacations in Chania, an ancient city on the northwestern coast of Crete.

Our family loved the Greek islands—Mykonos, Rhodes, Corfu, Skiathos, and, of course, Crete, not only because it's beautiful and the people there are so hospitable but also because it's the birthplace of my father and his younger brother.

The Cretan hospitality is epitomized by a man I'll never forget who did something for me that was way above and beyond the call of duty. It happened after our family had spent a couple of weeks in a small hotel in Heraklion, the capital of Crete, a city ninety miles or so east of Chania.

The evening before we were to check out of the hotel, I went to the front desk to pay the bill with my credit card. But the desk clerk told me that the hotel didn't accept credit cards. Fortunately, I had my checkbook with me, but when I offered to pay the bill by check, the clerk stopped me. The hotel did not accept checks, either, unless I had sent one in advance of our stay. He explained that it would take at least three weeks for them to receive the money from my bank.

It was too late at night to go to a local bank and try to work out a solution. So I went back to our room and explained the problem to Sara, who suggested that I call my office in the morning and ask them to wire some cash to the hotel. I would pay the company back as soon as I returned. But that was the last thing I wanted to do; I didn't want to expose my stupidity to management.

The next morning, I went to a local bank and asked whether they could cash a check. They had the same problem: it would take three weeks for them to receive the money from my bank.

As I walked back to the hotel, thinking of ways I could resolve the situation, I passed a store that sold auto parts and accessories. Because the company I worked for was heavily involved in that market, I decided to go into the store and talk to the owner. Maybe *he* would cash my check— after all, he would be very familiar with my company. In fact, he probably was selling some of our products.

Once inside, I greeted the owner and explained my problem. I handed him my business card so he would know I was legitimate and that my check wouldn't bounce. "You can call our offices right now," I suggested.

He smiled. "I'm calling nobody," he said, then opened a drawer full of drachmas. "Here—take whatever you need. I'll cash your check *ónta théli o Theós*" (God willing).

But this took place in Heraklion; it's not the story I wanted to tell you about Chania.

II

On another occasion, Sara and I traveled to Chania with my sister, my cousin, and her husband, Abram, a nice guy from Tunis who had dark skin and long ebony hair. He wore a mustache that covered his entire upper lip and went down to his chin.

We'd come across an article describing the restoration of Etz Hayyim, the only remaining synagogue in Crete, and we wanted to see it. So we decided to spend a few days in Chania.

After visiting the synagogue and the old Jewish quarter, where my father, my uncle, and their parents used to live, we spent the rest of our time shopping, sampling various foods, and exploring the city. I wanted to wear some traditional Cretan garb, so I bought a couple of *mandilis* and *kombolois* for Abram and myself—a *mandili* is a black crocheted kerchief with fringe around the edge that is worn around the forehead, and a *komboloi* is a string of beads with a tassel at the end that is held in the hand. We donned our *mandilis* and *kombolois* and went off to spend a few moments together—just us men—while our wives and my sister were shopping.

We found a table at an outdoor café in the center of the city and ordered a couple of Greek coffees. Abram and I were sipping our coffee and people-watching when a group of tourists, all blond women, got off a bus nearby and formed a circle around their guide. We noticed that a couple of them were staring at us.

The women whispered a few words to their guide, who hesitated for a moment, then approached us cautiously. He greeted us and politely addressed Abram in Greek. The women wanted someone to take a picture of them with genuine Cretans. Abram, who could not speak or understand a word of Greek, did not open his mouth. With his black hair, his long mustache, a *mandili* on his head, and a *komboloi* in his hand, he looked like a real Chaniote.

The guide was visibly rattled by Abram's silence. He had obviously been warned that Cretans have short fuses and carry long daggers. He apologized profusely, assuring us that he did not want to disturb us. He just was asking for a favor to please the tourists.

The guide then turned to me. "Can you please tell your friend that it will take only a minute?" I leaned toward Abram and said in Greek, with a pure Chanioti accent, "Afissetoús vré; móno éna leptó" (Let them, buddy; it will only take a minute). Of course, Abram couldn't understand me, either, but he got the idea that whatever the guide was asking was okay with me.

In the blink of an eye, the tourist women stood on either side of us. They giggled, happy to have a photographic souvenir with "genuine Cretans" that would impress their families and friends.

But I digress; that is still not the Chania story I wanted to tell.

III

After a few days in Chania, on that same trip with my sister, my cousin, and Abram, I had used up all the disposable cameras I had brought with me. I was hoping to find a place that carried them so I could buy some and take more pictures.

While my companions were busy browsing through souvenirs, I struck out on my own. There were stores lined up all along the narrow street where we were shopping. Most of the owners were busy with customers; others were trying to attract passing tourists.

Soon I spotted a disposable camera in the window of a small shop. The owner was sitting outside, dressed in typical Cretan clothes—wide-leg pants and a *mandili*, *komboloi* in hand—and reading a newspaper. He sported a carnation behind his right ear.

I greeted him in English and entered the store, hoping he would follow me. But the man did not budge. I went back to him, and this time greeted him in Greek. Without raising his eyes from the newspaper, he asked whether I really spoke Greek.

I told him I did. He then inquired how I had learned the language, so I told him that I had learned Greek from my father, who was born and raised in Chania.

He promptly jumped off his seat and embraced me. "What a great pleasure to meet a foreigner who speaks our language fluently—and with a Chanioti accent, no less!" With his arm around my shoulders, he escorted me inside his shop.

He apologized because he had only two disposable cameras. He took them from the shelf, put them in a bag, and handed them to me.

When I tried to pay, he stopped me. "This is my present to you. It's a great pleasure to see you maintain Chanioti tradition. Pass it on to your children!"

He gave me a strong handshake and said, "Na pass me to kaló" (Go with God's speed)—words I had often heard from my father when I was about to travel.

But again, this is not the story about Chania I wanted to tell you. The story about Chania is all about *sefté*.

IV

One year, during the children's summer vacation, Sara and I rented an apartment in Chania to get the feeling of living like locals for a couple of weeks.

For the first few days, I would accompany her to the market early in the morning. We enjoyed buying fresh food and preparing it for ourselves and our children. Sara knew exactly what to buy—I was basically along for the ride. I carried the bags and gazed at the merchants, the people, and the appetizing delicacies displayed in front of the stores.

But soon we realized that Sara was overwhelmed by the demands of keeping house and taking care of our children. I tried to alleviate her workload, but there were things she absolutely refused to let me handle.

We agreed that the one task I could manage was going to the market every morning and buying the things she needed to prepare the day's meals. She would write out a detailed list. After a few days, during which I proved to be up to Sara's standards, I allowed myself a little extra time while I was shopping to walk through the stores and watch the various scenes that unfolded in this microcosm of the larger world.

In my wanderings, I could not help but admire one particular store close to the market's entrance. It had all kinds of fruit artfully displayed near the front. There was also a delightful aroma emanating from the display's numerous baskets of apples, peaches, berries, and citrus. I was particularly interested in the ripe, succulent peaches—I wanted to taste them so much that I was practically drooling.

I picked up two peaches and went inside to pay. "How much do I owe you?" I asked the owner.

He didn't look happy. Was it for lack of business? He frowned at me and said, "Na pass sto thiáolo" (Go to hell).

I was shocked. What did I do to deserve this reception?

There was an empty chair close to his, so I sat down and, speaking in Greek, told him how much I'd admired his store from afar when I had gone shopping with my wife. Back then, I explained, I didn't have time to stop by. But now, I hoped to patronize his store regularly.

That seemed to calm him. He bagged the two peaches and took the money I offered from my hand. He said his name was Manoli.

By that time, though, there were around twenty people inside and outside the store, all ready to buy. The owner went from calm to exhilarated. He embraced me and kissed me on both cheeks. "Efharisto, efharisto pára polý!" (Thank you, thank you very much!)

I didn't understand the reason for the owner's profuse thanks, but I didn't bother to ask. He was too busy with all the customers he was attending to. As I was leaving, he ran to me and said, "Please come back tomorrow morning, Mr. Sefté."

Each morning thereafter, I would stop by Manoli's store, and the same thing would happen. As soon as I had bought my produce, a crowd of locals and tourists would stream in, all eager to buy the appetizing fruits he displayed out front. Manoli was certainly one of the happiest men in Chania.

A few days before the end of our vacation, on one of my daily visits, I suggested that Manoli hang a sign at the entrance to the market indicating that his store was located just inside. And indeed, when I went to Manoli's to say goodbye the day before we were scheduled to leave, I saw the sign. But this time, the store was already crowded. Manoli said, "You see, Mr. Sefté? Now I have a *sefté* hanging at the entrance to the market."

Later, I discovered that *sefté* has several meanings. Usually it refers to the first sale of the day. But there is a superstitious belief that the first sale can bring good luck or bad luck. That is why Manoli was so apprehensive about selling me only two peaches the first day I walked into the store.

Thankfully, now he has a permanent *sefté* on a sign hanging at the market entrance.

And that's the story I wanted to tell you about Chania.

The B-17 Pilot

I

Jeremiah Connor was the pilot of a B-17 flying over the Lombardy region in Italy in 1943. His mission was to destroy an ammunition plant in Campione d'Italia, an important supplier for the occupying German army. The plant was located high on a mountain and surrounded by forest.

The US air forces had lost many aircraft and many lives trying to accomplish that challenging mission. In addition, the bombers were under strict instructions to avoid dropping any munitions on Switzerland, just across Lake Lugano. They had to fly at very low altitudes and expose themselves to fierce German antiaircraft fire.

At the age of twenty-three, Jeremiah was considered one of the best pilots in the European theater. He had successfully carried out fifty missions in Berlin, Normandy, and Rome. But this was his first time flying a B-17 Flying Fortress. The plane was manned with ten men and loaded to capacity with bombs.

Jeremiah was born to devout Catholic parents. The family never missed Sunday Mass at the Cathedral of the Holy Cross in Boston. Even while serving in the air force in Europe, he would nearly always find a church where he could attend Sunday Mass, declining invitations to join other pilots at bars and brothels. And wherever he was, he said his prayers every night before going to sleep.

Jeremiah also loved Italian food. When he was a high school student in Boston, he worked every summer in one of the best Italian restaurants in town. He dreamed of saving enough money so that he could spend some time in Milan, the hometown of the restaurant's owner.

In fact, he was thinking about Italian food when the B-17's bombardier, sitting below him at the aircraft's nose, put on the red light, signaling that they were approaching the target zone. Jeremiah made the sign of the cross and started to lower the B-17 to the altitude specified by the bombardier. When the plane reached the target, he unloaded all the bombs in one strike.

"We got it!" the bombardier and the navigator shouted from below. The other members of the crew whooped and hollered in triumph.

But they didn't have much time to celebrate: the Germans on the ground had detected the B-17, and their powerful guns unleashed a hail of gunfire. It looked as though fireworks were exploding around them in the dark sky.

Jeremiah was frantically swinging the plane right and left to avoid the bullets while simultaneously trying to gain altitude and get the plane out of the Germans' reach. But then it happened: the B-17 was shaken by a loud noise. The German guns had hit it.

The plane lost its right wing. Only one of the four engines was still functioning. Fire was about to engulf the entire plane. Jeremiah immediately pulled the evacuation alarm. Only four of the ten crew members were still alive.

They lined up at the bomb bay in the egress position. Jeremiah pulled the lever to open it, and his men jumped out. He could see their white parachutes deployed underneath the plane. Now it was his turn. He made sure he had his parachute well packed and went to the open bomb bay.

He made the sign of cross, ready to jump, but suddenly a thick white cloud enveloped him. It spoke in a deep voice: "Jeremiah, you're a righteous man. I'm here to save you!"

Jeremiah was mystified.

"Jeremiah, we don't have much time. Make a wish—anything you want, any place you want to be. But only one."

Jeremiah was completely stunned and couldn't say a word.

The cloud was getting impatient. "Hurry up! I cannot hold the plane any longer."

"Milan!" was the only word he could come up with before he lost consciousness.

Jeremiah was awakened by ice water thrown in his face. He was lying on bushes that surrounded giant pine trees. He looked around and saw a group of people examining him for injuries.

Between the smattering of Italian he had learned at the restaurant in Boston and the broken English of the group's leader, they managed to communicate. The group had seen the plane crashing in the forest. They told him that the other members of his crew were shot down while still in their parachutes.

They were in a hurry to move because very soon German troops would be searching the area. They picked up his parachute and cleaned up the site, leaving no trace of his fall, and carried him to a truck parked near a dirt road.

They drove to a farm that belonged to the leader of the group. He and his three sons took Jeremiah to a barn filled with hay bales and farm implements. Inside was a hidden door to a secret room undetectable to inquisitive visitors. The room contained a bed, a dresser with a mirror, and a shower with a hole that also served as a toilet.

Jeremiah was told that besides being farmers, his rescuers were also *partigiani*—members of an Italian resistance group who fought against the fascist regime in Italy as well as the German occupying forces.

The leader's wife came into Jeremiah's hideout. She had been a nurse, but now she took care of wounded fighters, sometimes serving as doctor and surgeon. Her diagnosis was that Jeremiah was in good shape and could go about his normal activities. However, the consensus was that he should stay in the secret room for a couple of weeks, until the Germans had given up their search for him.

After two weeks had gone by, the family took him out of hiding. They gave him typical farmer's clothes and let him work with them on the farm in exchange for room and board. Jeremiah got along so well with the family that they took him to the nearby church for services—even though occasionally German soldiers searched the sanctuary for saboteurs and other potential enemies. The plan was that as soon as warm weather arrived, the family would take Jeremiah to the Swiss border, where he could escape safely and from there go back to the United States.

Sometimes the men of the family would go out at night and come back exhausted but happy. They would describe their exploits to Jeremiah: one time they blew up a bridge; another time they derailed a German ammunition train; on yet another occasion they threw grenades on a German convoy. They would invite Jeremiah to drink some good Italian wine with them as they celebrated their accomplishments. They also told Jeremiah that their farm was located halfway between Campione and Milan. And that Milan was considered the capital of the Italian Resistance.

Every few weeks, they explained, they would load their truck with vegetables, fruits, meat, and eggs and deliver the goods to a few of the best restaurants in Milan. On their way back, they'd stop at their arms and ammunition supplier. They would load the truck and hide the supplies under baskets, tools, clothes, and other objects.

When Jeremiah heard about the restaurants in Milan, he could not hold back. He told the family that he used to work in an Italian restaurant owned by a very kind and generous Milanese man. He also shared with them his love for Milanese food and his dream of spending time in Milan tasting the delights of the food in its native habitat, so to speak.

"Consider it done," they told him. "We'll take you with us on our next visit to Milan."

A week or so later, the family took Jeremiah to the best Italian restaurant in Milan, one owned by a good friend of theirs, also a *partigiano*. They told him about Jeremiah's adventure and his dream of tasting Milanese food in situ. The owner put his arm around Jeremiah's shoulder and took him to the kitchen, a cavernous room filled with gleaming high-end cooking equipment and what looked like miles of stainless steel fixtures and counters. It was a beehive of activity, with several cooks and assistants chopping and stirring and ferrying dishes to and fro. Everything was carefully orchestrated by Maestro Marcello, the *capo cuoco* (chief cook).

When Maestro Marcello understood why the owner had brought Jeremiah to the kitchen, he took him by the elbow and led him to a table in the corner. He asked him to sit: this was the place where Maestro Marcello examined every dish that came out of the kitchen. "I'll bring the best specialties here; we'll taste them with the appropriate wines. You'll eat the best food not only in Milan, not only in Italy, but also in the entire world."

Jeremiah spent three magical days in Milan sampling the most mouthwatering dishes—risotto alla Milanese, veal osso buco, costoletta, polenta, cassoeula—as well as Gorgonzola cheese and delectable pastries. He was still drooling when he told his new friends about his experience on their way back to the farm.

They had to wait until the beginning of summer for the snow to melt completely and a new moon to rise before they drove Jeremiah under cover of night to the Swiss border.

The farewells were short but heartbreaking. Jeremiah reassured the family that the American forces would soon defeat the Germans and the Italian fascist regime.

II

I met Jeremiah during a trip to my company's office in New York City. He was by then a seasoned executive running our very successful Peruvian operation. Right away we established a congenial, trusting, and mutually respectful relationship. He liked my straightforward personality. I appreciated his managerial skills and the way he treated his subordinates.

One evening when Jeremiah had occasion to make a business trip to Israel, where I was then working and residing, we had dinner at the King Solomon restaurant at the Tel Aviv Hilton. After we enjoyed our meal, Jeremiah ordered a Cognac and told me his amazing story. I already knew that he was one of the best bomber pilots in Europe during World War II, but I hadn't heard the complete saga of his rescue.

"Have you been back to Campione and Milan since then?" I asked.

Yes, he said, but only once, a couple of years after the war was over. The farm did not exist anymore, and the family who rescued him had vanished. Some said that they had been caught by the Germans and executed; others said they had escaped to Australia.

"And what about Maestro Marcello and the restaurant in Milan?"

Jeremiah took another sip of Cognac and sighed. "Unfortunately, there was nothing left of it. It was an empty storefront the last time I saw it. But I wish I could go to Milan again and experience more of the city's wonderful food. And maybe I could find Marcello at a different restaurant."

I thought, What a pity that Jeremiah is the regional manager of South America instead of Europe. At the time, Milan was my company's most important European outpost, home to our largest plant as well as our technical center.

So a few years later, as soon as I was in a position to do so, I promoted Jeremiah to manager of the European region. When I made the announcement at a sales conference, he was overjoyed. He came to me and whispered, "Now the wish I made to the cloud in 1943 is fully realized."

The Parrot

My company used to organize an annual cruise to an exotic destination as a reward for its best clients and its most successful managers. The presence of our chairman was a bonus: passengers could spend some quality time with him, and he in turn was happy to mingle and thank everyone for their performance and loyalty. One year, I was especially happy to be among the group of managers selected because the vessel's itinerary included Brazil, the country where our family had lived for many years, a place we truly loved.

The Brazilian leg of the journey ended in Manaus, where the ship remained docked for a few days. I was in good spirits, because as they did every year, Sara and our daughters, Hanna and Rahel, were spending the month of August in Greece. I missed them, but I was glad to know that they were relaxing and having a good vacation.

When the ship arrived in Manaus, instead of taking the guided tours of sites I had already visited many times, I decided to spend those days with my friend Sergio Soares, one of the wealthiest businessmen in the state of Amazonas.

Sergio had been my major customer when I worked in Brazil. I used to visit him twice a year and would stay in his sumptuous mansion in Manaus instead of a hotel. He greeted me warmly at the port, then took me to his junglelike ranch, around an hour away by car, where we spent our days lying in hammocks under large shady trees that bore all kinds of fruit.

When it came time for me to leave, Sergio took me to a bungalow on the property; he had a present for me. As soon as we walked in, I saw a large colorful bird flying around the room.

"It's an Amazonian parrot," Sergio said. The rainforest administrator, a friend of his, had given it to him. "It's a special male parrot, larger and more colorful than any they've seen. The authorities wanted me to have it. And now I want to offer it to you as a souvenir of the Amazon and of our friendship."

Sergio was very proud of his generous offer. But having a pet parrot was not at all in my plans. Besides, how would I get the bird back home? Could he withstand the remaining week of the cruise? Would he be comfortable in my cabin? Would he get seasick? Could he stand being stowed in a carrier on the airline afterward?

I tried to tactfully explain to Sergio that, while I appreciated his special gift very much, it was much better for the parrot to stay in his Amazonian habitat. And what would his forest administrator friend think about the parrot's disappearance?

But Sergio would have none of it; he was busy preparing the parrot for the journey.

The parrot freely entered a large cage equipped with swings, toys, wooden sticks, and containers for water and food. "Aren't you going to miss him?" I asked in a last attempt to get Sergio to change his mind.

"No. He speaks some kind of foreign language and gets upset when I can't talk back to him. You speak several languages; you two will get along fine."

Sergio took me back to the port in his chauffeur-driven limousine. He handed the cage with the parrot to his driver and asked him to take it onto the ship. Then he gave me a bracing farewell hug and said, "By the way, his name is Zephyr, but he prefers to be called Zeph."

To my surprise, Zeph behaved very well during the trip. In my cabin, I would let him out of his cage, and he would fly and hop around. Once in a while he would land on my shoulder and fix his gaze on me, probably trying to figure out what kind of person I was.

Somehow I managed to get Zeph safely back home. We had a small space off the living room that acted as my study, and I hung the cage there on a perch near the window. I also placed some sticks and toys around the room for him to play with when he was out of his cage. With the passing of time, he became more familiar with me, jumping on my shoulder and climbing on my back. But he had still not uttered a word.

When Sara and the girls came back from their vacation, they were thrilled to see our new guest, putting to rest any concerns I had—especially regarding Sara's reaction.

One Friday evening, Sara and I invited another couple over for Shabbat dinner. All evening, Zeph behaved like a true gentleman, even when our friends tried to tease him. He only craned his neck and perched on the top of his cage to better listen and observe us.

But he appeared agitated when I raised my glass of wine and said, "L'chaim." And at the end of the evening, when I saw our friends out the door with a "Shabbat shalom," Zeph appeared more agitated still.

Later that night, after Sara had gone to bed, I went into my study to see how Zeph was doing and make sure he was calm. As soon as he saw me, he flew over and sat on top of a filing cabinet. We were face-to-face. "So you are one of ours?" he asked in Hebrew, with a perfect Israeli accent.

I was speechless. Was I dreaming? Was this for real? How could a parrot speak such perfect Hebrew? Is this the language he spoke with Sergio, the one Sergio couldn't understand?

I answered that indeed I was.

"Your Hebrew is awful," Zeph told me bluntly. "You have an Arab accent. Where did you learn it?"

"In Egypt," I replied. "I attended a Jewish school in Cairo."

"Well, I guess it will do. I can finally communicate with someone who understands me."

I was getting used to this bird's somewhat disarming frankness. "Tell me, Zeph. Who are you? I mean, who are you really?"

"I am a rabbi who was turned into a magic parrot by certain divine forces who did not like my free-spirited personality. I've been looking for someone who will allow me to turn back into the rabbi I was before."

If I didn't believe in magic before, I believed in it then. "Are you under a curse?"

"Yes. A curse that can only be lifted through a wish made by a person like you."

"What do you mean?"

"It is within my power to grant one of three wishes for you. If you pick the right one, I'll immediately be transferred to Jerusalem as the most important rabbi in that holy city." With this, he gave a little ruffle of his feathers.

"Can you tell me beforehand which wish is the one that will set you free?"

"Of course not. If I cheat, I can turn into a worm or a snake."

"So let's hear what my choices are."

"First, you can wish for happiness. You can live twenty more years in total bliss, with no worries of any sort. You'll be able to do whatever you want without encountering any obstacles. But after you die, all your possessions will disappear.

"Second, you can wish for long life. You can live up to the age of 120. But your life will include illness and pain, and you will go through many unfortunate experiences.

"Third, you can wish for wealth. This will turn you into one of the richest men in the world. It will, however, take five years to reach the full extent of your wealth. And every one of those years will reduce your life span by three years."

Zeph must have guessed the skeptical thoughts going through my mind, because he pointed to a bottle of whiskey I kept on a bookshelf behind a glass door. "Just to prove that I have the powers I claim to have, I'll get that bottle over to you without either one of us having to lift it." He flapped his wings; the glass door opened, and the bottle floated slowly onto my lap.

"I believe you," I said immediately. "When do I have to give you my choice?"

He said, "By tomorrow before sunset. But tonight, let's drink some whiskey together. I'll sing some Hebrew songs that you probably know and teach you some others you don't know."

We sang and drank until the wee hours. When we had exhausted our repertoire, he flew back to his cage, and I went staggering to bed. However, I could not sleep for thinking about the three wishes Zeph was offering and trying to guess which of them would transform him into the rabbi he was before.

When she woke up the next morning, Sara looked at me. "You're pale; you haven't slept all night. What's going on?"

I replied, "Zeph has a problem. But I'll handle it."

I had my breakfast and then went to see Zeph, who was whistling joyfully. I told him that I was going out for a long run. Running had always helped me solve major problems I'd faced at work. I hope it would help, too, with the difficult choice Zeph presented me with.

Of the three wishes, I was leaning toward the first one, happiness, even if it meant a shorter life. And I was almost sure that it was the one that would liberate him from the curse. But did I really want a predestined life, even if every single moment was a happy one? Wasn't it better to experience life's ups and downs along with everyone else? And to preserve some of the mysteries of human existence?

The afternoon passed rapidly, and I still didn't know which option I was going to choose.

Zeph came out of his cage a few minutes before sunset. He seemed anxious. He flew over to me on the couch, where I was still wrestling with my decision. "It's time now for you to tell me your wish," he said.

I put my hand on his neck and caressed him.

"Tell me, Rabbi Zeph: What will happen if I have no wish?"

Tante Clarice

My maternal grandparents had nine children, one boy and eight girls. Tante Clarice was the youngest. They were all born and raised in Smyrna, a city that was once part of Greece but was occupied by the Turkish army in 1922. In 1930, its name changed officially from Smyrna to Izmir, its current Turkish name.

Sometime between 1915 and 1920, after the death of my grandfather, the remaining family members decided to emigrate from their homeland. Some went to Europe, others to South America. Clarice, her mother, and three of her older sisters went to Chile, where they lived in a suburb of Santiago. By the late 1990s, my siblings and I hadn't heard from Tante Clarice in many years; there were rumors among some of my cousins that she had gone mad.

My wife, Sara, and I, along with our two daughters, Rahel and Hanna, now lived in Tel Aviv in a large apartment located in a nice neighborhood. I had been promoted from president of our French subsidiary to vice president in charge of the Middle Eastern and African regions, a position that required frequent long trips overseas. Despite my demanding job, we were living a happy and comfortable life.

One Saturday morning I was relaxing on a chaise longue on our balcony reading a book. Sara had taken the girls to the park to play. I was calm and relaxed, enjoying the serenity of the day, when my cell phone rang. I picked it up, surprised to get a call on Shabbat.

The voice of a woman who seemed distressed was mumbling in a language I couldn't understand. I hung up.

My phone rang again. I picked it up and heard the same voice as before, but a bit calmer. I finally realized that it was Tante Clarice and began to piece together fragments of what she was trying to tell me.

It seemed that her husband had died a few months previously from a massive heart attack, and she didn't have anyone she could trust besides me. She was not on speaking terms with her sisters and their families. She was begging me to help her leave Santiago and immigrate to Israel. Apparently she was in fear for her life—the rabbi of her synagogue, she claimed, was trying to kill her.

"He tried to strangle me," she said. I could hear her taking deep breaths. "I've locked my door and don't let anybody in. I can't leave the house."

This was unbelievable. Was she delusional? A rabbi trying to kill someone in his congregation? Completely absurd, obviously a sign of severe paranoia or dementia.

Clarice interrupted my thoughts. "Avi, please. I'm alone here. I have no children. I have nobody, and I'm scared. Your mother was my favorite sister; she was the smartest and kindest among us. Everyone in the family speaks highly of you, so I know you take after her. Please come and take me back with you to Israel," she implored.

I told her that I had to think it over and promised to call her back soon.

Shortly after I finished my conversation with Tante Clarice, Sara came back from the park with our daughters. I told her that Tante Clarice had called and wanted me to help her move from Chile to Israel. I added that Clarice thought her rabbi was trying to kill her and that she must be experiencing some kind of mental breakdown. Sara listened patiently, and after thinking for a few moments, she said, "You cannot let Tante Clarice stay alone in Santiago in the state she's in. Bring her here to live with us."

I called Tante Clarice back and told her that I would soon travel to Santiago and bring her back with me.

Less than three days later, Clarice and I were on a plane en route to Tel Aviv. We went directly to our apartment, where I showed her to her quarters—a small furnished room, complete with a TV, a nice twin bed, and a large closet. She walked in, smiled, and said that it would be more than enough for her needs. "Thank you for all you're doing for me," she said while embracing our daughters.

As an *oleh hadash* (new immigrant), Clarice was granted full Israeli citizenship, including all rights and benefits.

We were glad to have her with us. The girls were happy because they could tell their friends that they had a "mamaw" living with them. Clarice also helped Sara in the kitchen, cooking Ladino recipes her family had prepared in Smyrna. She took Hebrew lessons and learned the language with amazing facility. She took care of the house when Sara and I were out. She babysat our daughters and even put them to bed, lulling them to sleep with stories and songs from "the old country."

However, around a year after Clarice arrived in our home, I noticed that the girls were not as cheerful and lively as they used to be. I asked Sara whether she knew what was going on. At first she didn't want to tell me. She didn't want me to worry about our home life while I was so busy at work. But she said that things had changed with Clarice. "She's acting like she owns the place!" Sara said.

I insisted that she give me more details.

In an anguished voice, Sara listed Tante Clarice's misdeeds in a long and uninterrupted monologue.

"She's started giving orders to the girls and even to me. She had a fight with our next-door neighbor. She complains that we don't have enough food. While you were traveling, she came to our bedroom in the wee hours, screaming at me because the girls took the last piece of watermelon. She suspiciously counts her money, and many times she's accused Hanna and Rahel of taking bills from her wallet. And now she's started to sow discord between the two of them, telling Hanna that Rahel is smarter than she is and Rahel that Hanna is more beautiful. I did not want to confront her about it. After all, I'm the one who asked you to bring her here."

I was shocked. I told Sara that I would be home every night for the next few weeks and would take care of the situation.

One night after dinner and putting the girls to bed, Sara and I continued talking at the dinner table. Then we went to our bedroom to retire for the evening.

I was deep in sleep when I sensed a presence in our room. I opened my eyes to see Clarice leaning over us, scrutinizing our faces. I jumped out of bed and snapped, "What are you doing here?" Clarice ran back to her room.

My question to Clarice had awakened Sara. I told her that the next day I was going to give Clarice a choice between going back to Santiago or moving into the nice retirement home in Jaffa that one of Sara's friends had chosen for her mother. The present situation was intolerable.

Early the next morning, I went to Clarice's room. I was surprised that she was still in bed and the curtains were drawn. She was moaning, doubled over, with her hands on her belly.

"I don't feel well, Avi," she said. "Something is wrong with my bowels. I had blood when I went to the bathroom!"

First I thought she was only pretending to be sick, seeking my sympathy, trying to avoid discussing what had happened the previous night. But when I opened the curtains and put the lights on, I saw that Clarice's face was pale and sweaty. Her lips were blue.

Sara and I decided to take her to the emergency room. We stayed with her while the doctors ran various tests. A CAT scan showed that she had some problems in her ileum; there was a suspicious spot close to the colon. They were keeping her overnight for more tests and would perform a colonoscopy the following morning.

Sara went to the hospital early the next day. Clarice had had the procedure and was recovering in her room. A few minutes later, the doctor arrived with an update. He said that there was indeed a spot on Clarice's ileum that may be cancerous. "We took a tissue sample for a biopsy and will get the final results in around three to four weeks. We will call you, then you can come to the hospital so we can discuss the results. We'll see where we go from there."

When she heard the word "cancer," Clarice began to tremble. "I'm going to die; I know it. God is punishing me for how badly I treated you and your daughters," she said to Sara. "I beg you to forgive me so that God will have mercy."

That night we all had dinner together. Clarice was even sweeter than she had been when she first came to live with us. After dinner, she stood up, put her hands together in genuine repentance, and said, "Please forgive me for all the pain I've caused you. I hope God will forgive me, too. I know I'll die from the cancer I have in my bowels, and I want to be at peace in my last few days." She kissed Hanna and Rahel and hugged Sara and me, tears streaming down her cheeks.

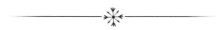

Over the course of the following weeks, Clarice was extravagantly affable, sweet, and helpful. She had undergone a complete metamorphosis, from she-devil to angel. Sara remarked, "You see what cancer can do to a person? We will forgive her and help her. She's adorable the way she is now."

We all knew that Clarice was in agony waiting for the biopsy results. We tried to help her by taking her out for dinner and to the park with the girls. Now the girls were the ones to put *her* to bed and sing the songs she had taught them.

Finally, the hospital called. Sara went with Clarice to hear the news from the doctor, who seated them in front of a screen in his office filled with images taken during Clarice's exams. He pointed with his pen at a dark shape: "This is the spot that worried us because it's in a critical area. If cancer is found in that area, it is life-threatening."

He paused, because he saw that Clarice was showing signs of a panic attack. He gave her a glass of water and put his hand on her shoulder. "Fortunately," he said, "the biopsy results are negative. No cancer, my dear lady!"

Clarice wept for joy. She stood and kissed the doctor, then turned to Sara and said, "Let's go home."

Over the next few days, Clarice continued her good behavior. Before going to sleep one evening, I said to Sara, "You're right. This episode was redemption for Clarice."

But that same night, after Sara and I had fallen fast asleep, I again woke up and felt a presence in our bedroom. I opened my eyes and saw Clarice scrutinizing Sara's face, almost touching her. I seized Clarice firmly by her arm and took her out of the bedroom.

"What's going on? Why are you intruding in our private life? What happened to all your promises?"

"Well, that was when I thought I had cancer. I'm well now. I need to do my thing and feel happy."

The next morning, I asked Sara for the name of that nice retirement home in Jaffa.

Selection

I've known Itay ever since I moved to Tel Aviv. I met him early one morning in the gym we both belonged to, an elite fitness club frequented by celebrities and other high-profile individuals. Membership in this club was one of the perks of my job.

At that hour, we were the only ones using the facility. It took us just a few moments of conversation to discover that we shared many of the same beliefs and principles. We both left the club feeling that we had made a new friend. We exchanged phone numbers and decided to meet one evening to have a longer and quieter discussion than was possible in the gym.

A few weeks later I invited him to join me for a drink at the Vista lounge in the Tel Aviv Hilton. At the time, he was continually in the news. Itay was the hottest bachelor in Israel, not only because he was the only Israeli athlete who succeeded in getting four gold medals at the World Aquatics

Championships a few years previously but also because he was considered the most handsome and sexiest young man in Israel. Among other exploits, he had set record times in the men's four-hundred-meter freestyle competition—way faster than any other swimmer.

It goes without saying that Itay was pursued by a host of women wherever he went, not only in Israel but wherever he happened to be competing. He always had a beautiful woman on his arm, but unfortunately, these relationships tended to last only one or two weeks at the most.

That evening at the Hilton, after talking about world issues and Israeli politics, we talked about our work. I told him about my job and the frequent trips I had to make around the world. He told me that he had retired from competitive swimming and was training and coaching the Israeli national swim team. "It's nice to train the younger generation," he said. "I hope a few of them will be able to beat my record."

I told him I was married with children and asked if he was, too. No, he was not married yet, he said. He wanted to settle down, but he hadn't found the ideal person. "After dating someone for a certain amount of time, I always discover some bad habits and annoying characteristics that I cannot tolerate in a person I'm going to live with 'until death do us part.'"

I was surprised. "Not even one person, with all the women who are after you?"

"Let me give you an example." He smiled. "Her name is Inga. It's a Scandinavian name that means 'peace and prosperity.'" He looked around to make sure nobody was within earshot. "The problem is that whenever we had sex, she could not help but pass gas. Loudly! I thought it was just a one-time phenomenon, an anomaly. But the same thing happened on each of the following nights. That's not the kind of music or perfume I want to live with."

I stammered, "Poor girl."

Itay grew serious. "Yes, poor girl. But what about poor me?"

I took a sip of my beer. Was he expecting me to offer advice?

Fortunately, he just wanted to share his romantic experiences. "I decided to prepare a questionnaire containing a list of behaviors and characteristics I cannot tolerate in a spouse." He said that of course he would not present this questionnaire to his potential wives—he'd merely talk about it as a kind of game.

I told him that seemed like a good plan and wished him luck.

A few months later, we met again at the Vista lounge. While we sipped our beers, I hastened to ask whether he had gotten married.

With a grin, he said, "Not yet, but I came close."

"What happened?"

He took a moment to respond. "Well, this woman passed the questionnaire test. She had none of the faults I had on my list. Everything was fine: she was gorgeous, intelligent, funny, passionate— everything I want in a wife."

"What went wrong?"

"Well, you know, we spent many evenings together. But none of them included sleeping in the same bed at night. After we had sex, she'd go home, and I would sleep alone."

I was still waiting.

He held his head in his hands and went on. "We decided to get married. A few days before the wedding, she slept in my bed because it was late." He took a deep breath and added, "But she snores. Not a light, tolerable snore but a snore that sounds like a train passing though the bedroom."

I couldn't stop laughing. I managed to ask, "Now what?"

"Well," he said, "I'll add snoring to my list. Maybe next time we meet I will have tied the knot."

"Inshallah," I replied.

Adam and Eve

Lord Ryweinster was one of the wealthiest billionaires in the UK. He owned a large mansion in an exclusive residential area of London populated by celebrities and tycoons. The Ryweinster home was featured in British media as one of the most luxurious in the UK.

A graduate of the University of Oxford and the Wharton School, Lord Ryweinster made his fortune as the founder and CEO of a top-performing hedge fund. He was extremely skilled at gauging the ups and downs of the volatile British economy in the 1970s and '80s. In addition, he had been knighted in recognition of the fact that he was one of the most generous philanthropists in England.

To understand global financial dynamics, Lord Ryweinster traveled frequently all over the world. It was during a trip to South America that he met his future wife, a Brazilian supermodel who was also a devoted Catholic raised by very religious parents.

It was love at first sight. She fell for this slender, elegant, and athletic man. He succumbed to the charms of this stunning, sensual woman with long jet-black hair and large green eyes. What's more, she spoke fluent English.

But after a few years, the flames of their passion began to die down. The heat was cooled by his increasingly demanding work schedule and her seemingly nightly participation in high-society galas and other events. They slept in separate bedrooms because they did not want to disturb each other when they were late coming home.

One day, on a plane flying home to England, Lord Ryweinster felt extremely tired— particularly tired, in a way that was different from the way he usually felt after one of his long trips. He had noticed this kind of tiredness a few months previously, but this time it was even more severe. He had had a fever, accompanied by profuse sweating, the night before he boarded the plane. He had also noticed that he was losing weight. He decided to see his doctor soon after his arrival in London.

Lady Ryweinster, meanwhile, felt neglected by her husband. Deprived of the passionate physical connection that had brought them together in the first place, she embarked upon a series of love affairs, most of them with men she met at the high-profile events she attended. Her conquests were among the most elite and famous personages in the arts and politics.

But Lady Ryweinster, too, noticed that she was not feeling well. She felt nauseated after her coffee in the morning and after her afternoon tea. She had to forgo meetings with her friends and skip her charity dinners. She also decided to see her doctor.

Both doctors had devastating news: Lord Ryweinster had AIDS, and Lady Ryweinster was three months pregnant.

Lord Ryweinster recalled that several months ago he had spent the night with a beautiful South African woman he had met at an exclusive supper club. Now he remembered that she had been trying to hide a persistent cough. He knew the moment he left the doctor's office that he had to avoid any sexual contact with anyone, especially with his wife—not only for the sake of her health but also to avoid the disastrous publicity the knowledge of his illness would create.

Lady Ryweinster, for her part, stayed a long time in her doctor's office, crying and repeatedly asking, "What am I going to do?"

The doctor, seeing how distressed she was, held her hand. "Let's go over your options," he said. "One, talk to your husband and tell him you are pregnant. Two, have an abortion. Three, go home and sleep with your husband as soon as possible."

The first option was out of the question. Her husband would throw her out of the house if he found out she was having affairs with other men. And an abortion was strictly forbidden by her religion.

She decided she would spend the night with her husband in his bedroom.

As soon as Lord Ryweinster arrived home, she stood up to greet him. He said that he had to take a shower and slipped away to his bedroom.

Lady Ryweinster waited a few minutes, then went to her boudoir to prepare for a night of erotic bliss.

A short while later, she appeared in her husband's bedroom, wearing her most revealing red silk negligee and an exotic, heady perfume. She held a bottle of Champagne in one hand and two crystal flutes in the other. She absolutely had to achieve her objective—that very night.

Lord Ryweinster was lying in his bed under heavy velvet covers. She walked toward him and placed the bottle and glasses on a round table. She slowly slipped under the covers and whispered all kinds of sexual suggestions in his ear.

At first he tried to tell her that he was tired and wanted to sleep, but this seemed to make her even more daring and provocative. It was a life-and-death struggle between a woman using her charm and feminine wiles to get what she wanted and a man who had to resist her at all costs.

Who would prevail? Lady Eve Ryweinster? Or Lord Adam Ryweinster?

Cannibalism

Absolutely, totally, I was against that trip. But Moti ended up persuading Eddie, and the two succeeded in persuading me.

Every year, the three of us would choose a place for a getaway—a spot where we could spend a few days together, have fun, and enjoy one another's company. But that year we had a hard time agreeing on a location. Because I was busy and uninspired, I had hoped Moti and Eddie would come up with some good ideas.

Eventually, they told me they had made up their minds. They were coming to Tel Aviv to spend the week of Passover at a kibbutz, and they wanted to stop by my apartment to show me the brochures and information they gathered about the place they had chosen. They were staying on a few more days after the Passover week so we could all travel to our destination together.

So we sat in my living room with the various materials spread out on the coffee table. But I couldn't comprehend what I was seeing: they wanted to go to Papua New Guinea.

I looked at them in disbelief. Were they kidding? Weren't there cannibals there?

No, they were not kidding. They were serious—especially Moti, who passionately described all the exciting things we could do there. "Look at these lush forests! We could hike through them, even get to meet some of the local tribes. We could stay in a tree house! Plus, they have some unexplored wild rivers there that are home to a wide variety of rare fish."

I was stunned, shaking my head.

Eddie chimed in. "It's really a unique trip—the kind of adventure that will remain with us for the rest of our lives."

"I still think it's a dangerous and crazy idea."

"Come on, Avi. Think of it as a birthday present for me," Moti added. "My special day is coming up, and if all goes well, we can celebrate while we're there. You know how much I love to fish."

Moti and Eddie got up to leave. "Read all these materials—they'll overcome any doubts you have. I'll call you tomorrow—we must make our reservations very soon," Eddie said in parting.

I must have been swayed by Moti's mention of his upcoming birthday. After all, I felt warmly toward Moti—he had been one of the most popular students in our class when the three of us were in school. He had all the qualities of an explorer—he belonged to a sports club that organized fishing competitions in Brazil and overseas and had won many first-place trophies. There is no doubt that he would be thrilled to go to Papua New Guinea.

After he and Eddie left, I read the materials they had brought. Most of them emphasized the modernization and even westernizing that had taken place in Papua New Guinea, especially among the Korowai tribe, who lived in the southeastern part of the country. The Korowai, the articles claimed, were selling forestry products and trading in rupiah, which had been introduced to them by missionaries. Many Korowai had converted to Christianity.

At least that didn't seem as frightening as the article I had read in *Smithsonian* magazine a few years previously—"Sleeping with Cannibals." The author claimed that the Korowai were still practicing cannibalism. Gulp.

When Eddie called the next day, I told him about the article. "That's sensationalism! The magazine just wants to attract readers. Things have changed now for sure. Don't be such a worrywart."

At last I accepted. There was an exclamation of joy on the other end of the line.

Moti and Eddie took care of all the arrangements. They booked the trip with an Indonesian tour company that specialized in such excursions. The round trip would last fourteen days.

Our journey started and ended in Djakarta. The first week involved two airline flights, trips by car and motorcycle, water crossings by boat and kayak, and long hikes. The second week was to be spent in Korowai territory so that Moti could catch the rare fish he was looking for.

This sounded like an adventure comparable to the Labors of Hercules. A nightmare! But I intended to at least be prepared and equip myself with everything I needed. I went to my doctor and got all kinds of vaccines and inoculations, along with antianxiety medication, sleeping pills, and painkillers. I also bought batteries and special chargers for my cell phone and smartwatch.

Two days before departure, I filled my extra-large rolling backpack with all my supplies. The night before, I took an antianxiety pill and a sleeping pill so I would be relaxed and rested when Moti and Eddie came to pick me up the next morning.

The doorbell rang twenty minutes before the agreed-upon pickup time. But I was ready. I hoisted my backpack over my shoulders, slipped a cap over my head, and jumped in the cab with my two longtime friends.

The first airline flight was uneventful and even fun. Moti and Eddie kept me entertained with jokes and reminiscences of our previous adventures. They wanted me to relax because they sensed that I was still apprehensive.

We slept in a nice hotel in Djakarta. The next morning, we flew to a place called Jayapura and from there to Dekai, a small town in the province of Highland Papua. We stayed in a small but very clean hotel. It looked like we were following the same itinerary as some of the explorers and journalists who wrote the articles and brochures I had read. Their tales impressed me so much that I reread them during our trip. Like many of those who visited Dekai before us, we were amazed by the remarkably modern and shrewd Manimo tribe. We promised we'd buy some of their souvenirs on our way back.

Each of us had specific skills that were useful to the team. Moti was intrepid, strong, and athletic. Eddie excelled in planning and organizing. I liked team sports such as basketball and soccer. I was also the intellectual one: reading and writing were among my favorite ways to spend leisure time.

On the morning when we were scheduled to travel to Korowai territory, Eddie was waiting for us at breakfast, fresh-faced and smiling. "In a few minutes," he said, "we are going to meet our two guides and take possession of some items I had shipped—camping gear and gifts for our new tribal friends. In fact, here are our guides now." He hurried over to meet and shake hands with two bare-chested men.

"This is Vic," Eddie said by way of introduction. "He is the best translator in the area, because he is fluent in the many languages spoken in this country. He is also friendly with a few of the Korowai families we'll be visiting soon. And he's a fine cook."

Vic was short and chubby—the opposite of his companion, Moses, who was tall, lean, and muscular.

Eddie then explained that Moses was the best tracker around. He knew all the trails in the dense Korowai forest. "He'll be carrying the heavy loads, and he'll be sailing the boat we use for transportation and fishing," Eddie explained.

Sensing that we were beginning the tough part of our journey, I swallowed two antianxiety pills.

Then off we went. We rode in old beat-up cars and even motorcycles on rough roads. There were times I thought my torso would be torn off at the hips. Nonetheless, we made it over the roads and onto a boat on which we sailed for what seemed like hours to the village of Mabul.

I noticed that Moti and Eddie were getting tired and somewhat concerned. I, on the other hand, was calm and relaxed, thanks to the pills I had been swallowing during the journey. I felt groggy, as if I had been receiving strong opioid injections. There was a light cloud screen in front of my eyes, but I could still admire the deep green forest and the peace of the jungle as we floated along the river.

I remember that we lodged for several days with a Korowai family. We had to climb a tall tree to enter the house. Vic's skill as a translator was invaluable. During the day, we would go out with Vic and Moses to explore the forest. We had to be back early in the afternoon to have dinner, because the Korowai went to bed before sunset.

One very early morning, while I was still half asleep, I saw Moti and Eddie leave the house with Moses. They carried their fishing gear, ready to troll the rich fishing waters. But I did not feel up to joining them. So I stayed behind and spent the day alternating between helping Vic cook and playing with the children. Vic prepared his specialty: rice with river fish, to which he added bananas and sweet potatoes. The children were completely absorbed by the toys we had offered them. The boys were amazed by the windup car that kept going, rolling and turning around, whenever it hit an obstacle. The girls were having fun wearing the necklaces, bracelets, and rings we had given them. You could hear their giggling and laughter all over the house.

After dinner, darkness started to fall upon us. We had to get ready to sleep. But I was worried about Moti and Eddie, who hadn't returned. Where were they? Vic did not seem to share my concern. "Moses knows the forest better than any other guide," he said. "They'll be here soon. Go to bed; I'll wait up for them." Because I had taken my sleeping pills, it didn't take long for me to plunge into a deep sleep.

I was suddenly awakened by a commotion in the house, accompanied by loud sobs. In the glow of the rising sun, I could see Moses in the arms of the head of the Korowai household, both men howling like wounded animals, tears streaming down their cheeks. Vic stood nearby, his hands covering his face.

"What's going on?" I asked. "Has something happened to the children?" I peeked at the corner where they slept, but they were all present and accounted for.

Vic led Moses to a tub of water and washed his face and arms, which were covered in blood, mud, and scratches. "They were killed . . . and eaten," Vic sputtered.

It took me a few seconds to understand what he meant. Was he talking about my dear friends Moti and Eddie? I wanted to ask questions, but my mouth couldn't form the words.

Vic saw that I was in shock, so he scooped a cup of water from the tub and threw it in my face. That brought me back to my senses. I asked Moses a million questions: How? Where? Who? And one particularly pointed inquiry: "Why didn't you save them? You were supposed to guide them and protect them!"

Moses was on his knees, his arms outstretched, begging for forgiveness.

Vic said, "Before blaming Moses, let's hear the story in his own words."

Moses took a deep breath and began. "At first, we had a nice ride on the river. Moti and Eddie caught some rare fish. They were both excited and happy. However, after a while, Moti wanted to go farther down the river, crossing into areas that were not safe.

"I tried to dissuade him, to no avail. Even Eddie insisted that we turn the boat around and come back here. But Moti was in ecstasy: he was sure that very soon he would be able to catch a big fish—the one he said was the rarest in the world.

"The river took us through some sharp turns. Eddie and I were begging Moti to listen to us when suddenly we came face-to-face with dozens of unfriendly Korowai. They were standing on the shoreline, their bows and arrows pointed at us. They commanded us to come ashore, then they tied us up and took us to a clearing in the forest.

"I immediately understood that they were a band of Korowai isolated from the rest of the community. The father of the person who seemed to be the leader of the group had died the evening before, and other members of the tribe were getting sick. They were looking for the *khakhua*—the witch—responsible.

"As we watched, the tribe was making preparations for a feast. Suddenly, the leader took hold of Moti and Eddie, placed them facedown over a flat rock, and chopped their heads off with a sharp stone ax. I saw this with my very own eyes.

"But while the rest of the tribe was continuing their preparations, I was able to slip away unnoticed. Before disappearing into the jungle, I noticed that several tribesmen were cooking what looked like large pieces of meat wrapped in banana leaves over a roaring fire.

"It took me more than nine hours to walk and crawl through the mud all the way back here, fighting leeches, mosquitoes, and thorny tree branches the entire time."

Then Moses looked at me and said, "Sir, your friends were eaten by cannibals, and I could not save them!"

My head was spinning, and I collapsed.

I had the vague feeling that I was carried away by boats, cars, and planes. Somehow, I arrived back at my own house in the late afternoon. Sara wasn't home, fortunately, so I didn't have to explain to her what had happened to Moti and Eddie just yet. I fell into a deep, comalike sleep, mentally and physically exhausted.

Early the next morning, Sara rushed into our bedroom and shook my shoulder. "You're still asleep? Hurry! Moti and Eddie are waiting in the cab."

"No way," I answered. "They were eaten by cannibals."

I turned over on my other side and went back to sleep.

Madly in Love

My friend Yosi and I spent several years together as high school classmates in Cairo. Subsequently, he immigrated to Israel and I to Brazil, where I took a job that required many overseas trips. Whenever I was in Tel Aviv, if time allowed, we would get together at the Vista lounge, on the top floor of the Hilton, a place where I often held business meetings.

Yosi was among my good and trusted friends. I liked his humor, his honesty, and his spontaneity. You didn't have to wonder about where you stood with him: he made his deepest feelings known without filtering them.

One evening, we were having a drink at the Vista and catching up on recent events in each other's lives. He had not married yet. He couldn't, he said, because he was madly in love with a unique woman who was unattainable. She had all the attributes of a Dulcinea—perfect in his eyes.

But she was always surrounded by an entourage—various hangers-on; celebrities and celebrity wannabes; the rich and famous. "She moves in a different orbit," Yosi said. "She is unreachable to people like me."

I was extremely curious. "What's her name? Have you met—"

He held up his hand and brought his chair closer to mine. "Her name is Nadia. She's Lebanese—very beautiful, with big black eyes and long wavy black hair. She fled Lebanon because of all the harm that Hezbollah was inflicting on her country."

He described her with passion, emphasizing each point with his hands. His eyes lit up: he was transported in ecstasy. "She is very well known all over the world," he continued. "She has been interviewed many times in Israel and other countries. She's been hosted by members of the Knesset as well as the president and prime minister." Apparently Nadia was brilliant as well as beautiful. She had gotten a doctorate in cardiology from a university in Beirut, followed by a research fellowship in Zurich. Recently, however, she spent most of her time campaigning against Hezbollah and other terrorist groups. Oh, and she was an actress, too—she had been cast as a Mossad agent in a popular Israeli TV series.

Yosi was ready to launch into another long monologue when he suddenly looked over my shoulder and froze. His mouth was wide open, and his eyes were ready to pop out of their sockets.

"What's the matter?" I asked. I moved my chair, ready to turn and look at what Yosi saw behind me.

He put his hand on my arm. "It's her. It's Nadia," he said under his breath. "Turn around slowly—do it discreetly so she won't notice. Drop something on the floor and then turn around to pick it up."

I followed Yosi's instructions. I saw a group of people who had just entered the lounge—a few men and a beautiful woman. They were seated at a table in a far corner so they wouldn't be disturbed.

He whispered, "That's Nadia. The government must have rented her a room at the Hilton until she can establish permanent residency here." Tears filled his eyes. "How lucky I am to be this close to the woman of my dreams!" His outpouring of emotion would have been funny if I didn't know he was deadly serious. I could see that he was in a very vulnerable state.

"Okay, listen, Yosi," I said. "You can't go on like this. You have to approach Nadia and at least let her know that you're a fan. She'll probably be flattered. You owe it to yourself to try."

"But how? How am I going to get through her flotilla of bodyguards?"

"Well, I bet that, like most people who stay here, she enjoys hanging around the pool. It's a good place to see and be seen. So why don't you come here on Saturday afternoon? Maybe Nadia will make an appearance poolside, and we'll find a way you can talk with her. Meanwhile, try to come up with another idea."

"Okay. I'll try. I'll be praying for a way to make my dream come true." He stood up and gave me a strong and long-lasting handshake. "You're really a mensch."

He left the lounge, but I stayed, still thinking about the best approach for talking to Nadia.

Yosi called me early Saturday afternoon. We met in the lobby, then changed into our swim trunks and went to the pool. We sat on lounge chairs under the shade of two large umbrellas and ordered some cold drinks. Then we waited, hoping Nadia would show up.

Yosi was trying to hide how anxious he was. Once in a while he would stand up, look around, and sit back down. He repeated this many times. Finally he stood up, groaned, and put his hands on his chest. "She's here! She just arrived!" He was almost hyperventilating. I told him he had to calm down and think about his next move.

Nadia's bodyguards prepared her a table at the edge of the pool, a spot where the general public was not allowed. She was wearing a revealing bikini, but the two men who accompanied her were in military uniform, complete with maroon berets. "They must be Sayeret Matkal," Yosi said—the equivalent of Special Forces in the United States.

After a few minutes, he told me that he wanted to take a walk around the pool. "I need to think," he said, then left.

A long time passed, and I was beginning to get concerned. I stood up to look for him. Then I saw him walking close to the table where Nadia and her bodyguards were sitting. Suddenly, he took two steps forward, stood at the edge of the pool, and jumped, trying to perform a double somersault in the air before diving into the water. But he missed. He landed at the edge of the pool, hitting his head on the coping tiles, and then plopped like a fish into the water.

There was a loud scream. People in and alongside the pool rushed over to help. I ran to the edge, ready to jump in and rescue him. Fortunately, two young swimmers had caught him on his way down, before he hit the bottom of the pool. They brought him out of the water and laid him almost at Nadia's feet.

Yosi was bleeding from a cut on his forehead. But the serious concern was that he was unconscious. Nadia instantly knelt and checked his heart. She raised her head and asked one of her bodyguards to call an ambulance. Then she immediately initiated CPR. A lifeguard joined her. She was administering mouth-to-mouth resuscitation while the lifeguard was doing chest compressions.

After a long, agonizing time, Yosi opened his eyes. The first thing he saw was Nadia's smiling face. They exchanged a few words, then I saw Nadia jump into the ambulance with him. Before it sped off, I managed to ask the driver which hospital they were taking him to.

That evening, I called the hospital and was glad to learn that Yosi was doing well. He needed several stitches on his forehead, but the wound would leave no scar, I was told. He would be discharged in the next few days.

I went to the hospital on Sunday morning to visit. Yosi was in high spirits. It was the most cheerful I'd ever seen him in all the years I'd known him. He was beaming with joy.

"Avi, yesterday was the happiest day of my life," he said. "Diving into that pool was the best thing that ever happened to me. And you, brother, were the one who made it all possible."

"But a double somersault, Yosi? At your age?"

"Well, as you'll recall, I used to do it in high school, and I thought I would be able to do it yesterday. But thank God I failed. I felt Nadia's kisses; I was in Gan Eden. And she asked me for my phone number because she wants to call me to see how I'm doing after I get home!"

We both laughed.

"Fate works in mysterious ways," I said.

The Mermaid

I sat on a bench overlooking the ocean at the edge of Monterey Bay. It was the best place for me to rest after a long morning run.

I was in California for a week on business. My company had assigned me to handle an important cybersecurity program for the Monterey Bay National Marine Sanctuary.

I stretched my feet in front of me, put my arms behind my head, and let my spirit get lost in the infinite horizon.

A man sat on a bench a few feet away from me, and when he spoke, he startled me out of my reverie. I glanced at him. He was a middle-aged man with a salt-and-pepper beard and mustache that covered his whole face. He was stammering a few words I couldn't make out. I wondered whether he was talking to me. It sounded as if he was speaking in a mixture of Hebrew, Arabic, and English, and eventually I realized that he wanted to initiate a conversation.

He walked toward me and sat down on my bench. He asked me a few questions—I told him my name was Avi and that I was spending a week in Monterey on business. When he was sure I wasn't a law enforcement officer, he opened a brown paper bag and took out a bottle of bourbon. "Go ahead, take a sip," he offered. When I declined, he slid closer to me on the bench.

He told me that he was a retired Israeli army officer on a monthlong vacation with his twelve-year-old daughter. His wife had died a few months earlier in a horrible car accident. He was waiting for his daughter to join him there at the edge of the bay.

He wanted to have a longer chat, but it was time for me to leave, so I stood up and shook his hand. His name was Nemrod.

"Enjoy the ocean view," I said, pointing at the binoculars at his side.

"I use them every morning . . ." His voice broke, and he wiped tears from his eyes.

I patted his back, trying to comfort him. I told him I was sorry I couldn't stay longer.

"That's okay," he said. "It's a long story I can share with you tomorrow morning if you're interested. But if you want to hear it, come an hour earlier."

The encounter with Nemrod had faded completely from my mind by the time I went out for my run early the next morning. But when I got close to the place where I had been sitting the day before, I saw Nemrod on the bench waving at me. I had to stop and forget about my run.

Nemrod had his brown bag and binoculars. This time he did not offer me a sip from his bottle of bourbon. He was rather in a hurry to tell me his story.

His family had immigrated to Israel from Russia just after World War II. His father found a job in the diamond district of Ramat Gan. At night, he trained with the Maccabi Tel Aviv water polo team, a sport he had practiced in Russia. His mother, a famous synchronized swimmer in Russia, taught ballet to young girls and initiated a synchronized swimming team in Tel Aviv. Both father and mother were avid swimmers and liked to spend time at the city's pools and beaches.

Nemrod fought in the Six-Day War, in 1967, and in the Yom Kippur War, in 1973. After several years as a bachelor, he finally met a Druze woman named Amal in a Tel Aviv swimming club. They married and had a girl they called Meryl.

Meryl was her parents' pride and joy and an excellent swimmer. At her school, she held the record in the two-hundred-meter breaststroke and hundred-meter butterfly competitions. She was a happy kid.

The car accident happened on a rainy evening when the family was driving back home from a swim meet where Meryl had earned several victories. She was in the back seat, and her mother was in the passenger seat.

Meryl was telling her mother that she didn't want to finish school. She just wanted to find a job as a lifeguard. This, of course, sparked a long and heated discussion between the two.

At this point in the story, Nemrod paused. I wasn't sure he would be able to go on. He was trying to hold back the tears that were welling in his eyes.

Finally he managed to say that there was a head-on collision with a truck. Amal was killed on the spot, while Meryl escaped miraculously with some minor scratches on her back and arms. Nemrod was taken to the emergency room with a large laceration that went from his right hip down to the bottom of his leg, a wound he was still caring for.

He spent several weeks in the hospital while Meryl was taken care of by an aunt. After his release, he decided to take Meryl on an extended vacation so they could get away from Tel Aviv and the inquisitive questions from relatives, friends, and even people they had never met. They both chose Monterey because of the National Marine Sanctuary and the beautiful weather. Meryl loved swimming in cold water, too, and she was told that the Pacific Ocean water in Monterey was much cooler than the water in the Mediterranean Sea at Tel Aviv.

They liked to take long walks on Monterey's beaches. But although Meryl always wore her bathing suit, during the first few days Nemrod did not want Meryl to swim in the ocean because the water was too cold. Also, there were boulders dotting the shoreline. Who knew how many more there were under the water? He had become very protective of his daughter after Amal's death.

Nemrod took a sip from his bottle, then swept his mouth with the back of his hand. "Meryl is a very sweet girl, very sensitive," he said. One day, as they walked along the beach, he was holding Meryl's hand. They saw people playing in the water not far from them. Suddenly, Meryl stopped and tried to free herself from her father's grip. He didn't let her go. She screamed, "Dad, that old man is drowning!" Nemrod looked at the man, who was surrounded by kids and adults. He told Meryl that the man was probably playing with his grandchildren. "He can't drown with all those people around him," he said as he dragged her away from the scene.

They continued walking for a few minutes, then they heard loud sirens. They circled back to see what was going on. An ambulance was parked at the same spot where Meryl had noticed the old man. When they got closer, they saw the rescuers carrying the man on a stretcher into the ambulance. He was gasping for breath. As a crowd of onlookers assembled, the man's son-in-law explained that no one had noticed that his father-in-law was drowning. He was the one who saved him.

Meryl was disappointed and angry for a couple of days after that, because she wanted to have been the rescuer. Then she became quiet and lethargic. To distract her, Nemrod took her to the Monterey Bay Aquarium. He also took her to see *Splash*, a movie in which Tom Hanks falls in love with a mermaid. Nemrod asked what she thought about the movie. After a while Meryl said she wanted to be a mermaid. Nemrod found her answer funny.

As the days passed, Meryl became more interested in wild ocean animals than in trying to save human lives on the beaches. When she was in the middle of reading a book about sharks and whales, she asked her dad to take her to a place where she could watch them. After making some inquiries, they chose the bench where Nemrod and I were sitting.

They spent many hours watching the ocean through the binoculars, and one day they finally spotted a couple of whales on the horizon. It happened at six in the morning.

Nemrod stopped his narrative momentarily to look at his watch. I automatically looked at mine; it was not six yet.

Nemrod could not find the words to describe the amazing scene that unfolded in front of them that day. Two whales exhibiting their power and grace just for the two of them—no one else was at their spot at that time of day.

Nemrod thought that maybe it was a mother whale with her calf, but Meryl didn't think so. To prove he was right, Nemrod drew Meryl's attention to the spout of water blowing out from the whale's back. The smaller whale had no spout—at least none that could be seen from that far away.

Meryl's loud laugh pealed through the air. Nemrod hadn't heard such a sound from Meryl since before her mother's death. That was not water, Meryl said, correcting him. What he was seeing was the whale's warm breath condensing into a cloud when it hit the cold ocean air. "Isn't it amazing that a twelve-year-old girl should know so much?" he asked me. "Were you aware of that?"

I shook my head; I just wanted him to go ahead with his intriguing story.

Nemrod took another sip of bourbon, and before he put it back in the bag, I took the bottle gently from him and risked a couple of sips myself, something I'd never done in my whole life—certainly not at such an early hour of the morning.

Nemrod's voice and face had changed. He was in a sort of trance. His eyes were moist, and they were fixed far away, on the ocean and the clouds.

He continued his story in a monotone. "We came here again at the same early hour every day, hoping to see the whales as we had the previous times. One day Meryl excused herself to use the women's room." Nemrod stopped.

After a while, I asked, "And?"

"And she did not come back," Nemrod replied. "I waited and waited, but there was no sign of her and no reports of any kind from the police or from beachgoers. She disappeared."

106

He rubbed his eyes and continued. "I came here again on my own the next morning, hoping to find her. At six, I automatically looked for the whales, as I had done with Meryl. They showed up, but this time there was something different.

"They were much closer to the shore than they had been before, and there was something between the two whales. I looked with my binoculars, and I saw a shape like a silhouette with a long tail swimming with them. Maybe a dolphin, I thought. But when I adjusted the binoculars, I could see Meryl swimming her impeccable butterfly stroke next to those gorgeous animals. It was her, I swear. She's a mermaid. And that's why I come here every day at the same time to watch her and hope that very soon she will come ashore."

I could not believe the end of the story. Meryl must have run away from her father. Or maybe she was abducted by a drug addict or drowned off some faraway beach. Nemrod was not normal, obviously. He was an alcoholic who suffered from delirium.

I was ready to go, but Nemrod stopped me. "Please stay a few more minutes," he begged. "It's six o'clock, and we can watch the whales together."

Nemrod picked up his binoculars and pointed his finger at the ocean. I could see the whales with my naked eyes. They were gliding and diving, their tails lashing the water. The mother whale and her calf—if that's what they were—were discernible, but there was also a third presence I could barely make out.

I was on edge. I grabbed the bottle of bourbon from Nemrod's hand and took several sips, then passed it back to him.

"It's Meryl," Nemrod kept repeating. He passed me his binoculars.

I raised them to my eyes and carefully adjusted them. The mother and calf, with their glistening black-and-gray skin, were distinctly visible. But there was that other something that was swimming between them. When I looked again, I could perceive a girl's face with long black hair stretching down her back.

"Does Meryl have black hair?" I asked.

"Yes, like her mother," Nemrod hastened to answer.

I don't know whether it was the effect of the bourbon, but I did see a young girl swimming beautifully between those two whales.

"Do you believe me now?" he asked.

I nodded.

"You believe she's a mermaid, right?"

"Yes." I nodded again.

"I'll be here every day until she comes back," Nemrod said firmly, expecting my encouragement.

I was mesmerized. "I hope she does come back," I whispered.

I flew back home early the next morning. Ultimately, I felt sorry for Nemrod. Was he suffering from delusions? From alcoholism? And did he succeed in dragging me into his fantasy world with his pathetic story and his bottle of bourbon?

And yet I can't deny it: I saw a young girl with long black hair swimming with the whales.

The Ultimate Fight

Arnold was the best mixed martial arts fighter America had ever seen. His supremacy was undisputed—no one else came close to having his level of power and skill. He had won numerous championships over the course of a decade. Women swooned over him. He was treated with respect everywhere he went. The ultrarich wanted him at their dinner tables; famous socialites wanted him at their galas. Money, acclaim, Champagne followed him wherever he went. The world unfolded at his feet.

He married Bridget just a year before he retired from competition. He was forty; she was thirty. They met at a dinner in New York City hosted by one of his sponsors. Bridget, a gorgeous blonde, was a professional dancer. She was there with a movie director who was interested in giving her a role in his upcoming film.

Bridget and Arnold's attraction was instantaneous; she ditched the movie director, and she and Arnold left the dinner together and enjoyed a wild, passionate night of lovemaking. They married a few days later.

One summer evening, after they had been married for a few years and Arnold had retired from competition, he and Bridget were heading home after a pleasant dinner at a friend's house in Short Hills, New Jersey, only slightly more than a two-hour drive from their home in northwestern Connecticut.

On the return trip, Bridget had to drive because Arnold had had a few drinks too many. Arnold didn't feel like arguing. Besides, Bridget was only too happy to drive Arnold's Bentley Continental GT convertible, which she wasn't able to do unless Arnold was away.

At that late hour, the expressway was almost deserted. The dark road stretched out in front of her. She unleashed the Bentley's horsepower and breathed deeply, filling her lungs with the perfumed night air. She also played classical music through the car's state-of-the-art sound system. Arnold was dozing, lulled by a Beethoven string quartet. Once in a while he would open his eyes and murmur sweet nothings to Bridget. "What a beautiful summer night," he whispered at one point before falling back asleep.

And then there was a bright white light . . .

Frank was a freelance sportswriter whose articles appeared in most of the country's popular newspapers and magazines. Although he covered many sporting events, martial arts were his favorite. He had followed Arnold's career for several years and interviewed him many times. Arnold had even invited Frank to his and Bridget's wedding and the celebrations that followed. Frank wasn't close to the couple, but they were more than acquaintances.

Frank was having breakfast when he heard about the accident on television. Arnold's Bentley had been hit by an eighteen-wheeler on the highway the previous night.

He and Bridget were taken to a nearby hospital. Initial medical reports indicated that Bridget had a concussion and superficial wounds. She was listed as stable. However, Arnold was unconscious and in critical condition.

Frank went to see him at the hospital a few weeks later, when he was out of intensive care. Bridget was there with Christian, a handsome young MMA fighter whom Arnold used to mentor.

Arnold did not want to elaborate on his condition, but Frank managed to find out that he had suffered several broken ribs and that after many examinations the doctors had discovered that he needed surgery to repair severe aortic valve damage.

Arnold had lost a lot of weight. He looked tired and weak and could only whisper in short sentences. "I'll be all right, Frank," he said, putting an end to his friend's inquiries.

On his way out of the hospital, Frank saw Bridget holding hands with Christian at the end of the corridor. When the two saw Frank, they hastily moved apart. "Christian is a good friend of ours. He's worried, and he's been trying to comfort me," Bridget mumbled as Frank stopped to say goodbye. Then she added, "Please come and spend time with Arnold when he is out of here. He likes you."

Frank promised to do so. But after reaching the elevator, he looked back at them; they stood close to each other, holding hands again.

Several weeks passed, and Frank did not go to see Arnold and Bridget as he had promised. He was quite busy with his job and did not feel like intruding in their lives. He justified this by telling himself that Arnold had fully recovered and was doing well.

One evening, Frank found a large brown envelope in his mailbox. It was a thick sheaf of papers from Arnold, written in longhand. Frank took his shoes off, lay back on the sofa, and propped himself up on a big puffy cushion, ready to read. Had Arnold written a novel? Could be very interesting!

But from the very first lines, Frank knew he wasn't reading fiction: Arnold was going through a horrible time. He described in detail the events that took place after he was discharged from the hospital.

His heart had taken a turn for the worse after the surgery. In addition, tests revealed that he suffered from an advanced case of pulmonary hypertension. He was put on the list for a heart transplant, which the doctors were reluctant to perform because of his poor health. But it was the only alternative. Meanwhile, he was ordered to stay home and follow a strict regimen of bed rest and healthful eating.

But the most touching and saddest part of the letter concerned Bridget and Christian.

They were having an affair in Arnold's own house. When Arnold came home, he found out that Christian had taken up residence in a guest bedroom. He and Bridget slept there together. But with the passing of time, they became more daring, kissing and fondling each other shamelessly in front of Arnold. The house was worse than purgatory. He could do nothing; his precarious health did not allow him to react or complain. It was hell!

He spent many sleepless nights fighting suicidal thoughts and imagining the perfect way to kill the couple. On one line he had scrawled in large capital letters: I CAN'T TAKE IT ANYMORE!

Arnold ended the letter by asking Frank for a favor. "Come to my house on Sunday morning at eleven o'clock sharp," he wrote. "Go directly to our backyard and be prepared to witness an exceptional event."

It took Frank a long time to absorb the contents of the letter and recover from the emotional shock. He could not imagine the Arnold he knew—the champion whose opponents trembled at the sound of his name, the man who was respected by the rich and famous and adored by his fans—reduced to a frail shadow of himself and imprisoned in a useless body. Frank decided to comply with Arnold's request and try to cheer him up on Sunday.

On the appointed day, Frank was dismayed to find that seemingly everyone in New York had decided to take the same route to Connecticut as he did. Traffic was crawling, and it was almost noon when he drove through Arnold's gate.

His heart skipped a beat when he saw an ambulance and a fire truck in the driveway, lights flashing.

Bridget ran to Frank's car, out of breath. She tried to explain what had happened: she was busy in the kitchen preparing lunch when she saw Arnold and Christian heading to the backyard with MMA gloves in their hands. She thought Arnold was going to teach Christian some of his moves.

But when they did not show up for the meal, she went to the backyard and saw Christian checking Arnold's pulse. Arnold was lying motionless on the grass. "I called 911 a few minutes ago," he told her.

Just as Bridget finished her story, she and Frank saw paramedics carrying Arnold to the ambulance on a stretcher, covered with a blanket. They looked at Bridget and Frank. One of them pointed to his chest, signaling that Arnold's heart had failed. He was certainly dead.

Frank turned his car around and headed home, wanting to be alone. Arnold had found the best way to commit suicide—while fighting his last fight. He died performing the sport he loved . . . and defending his honor.

Frank never watched another mixed martial arts competition again.

My Resourceful Friend

When Eddie, Moti, and I attended the Jewish Community School in Cairo, we became friends with Joe, a resourceful guy who liked to hang out with us.

Joe wasn't interested in studying or in any of the school's extracurricular activities. Still, he was very popular. He could get you anything you needed. If you were in panic mode because you forgot your pen, your eraser, or a book, for example, all you had to do was go to Joe. He would find a way to get it for you—for a price. And that price was in direct proportion to the extent of your anxiety.

One day I forgot to do my French homework. I had been told to write a brief essay describing my cat. As we all filed into the classroom and took a seat, I realized in a flash that I had nothing to hand in. My stomach turned over. In around ten minutes, the teacher would enter the classroom and collect our homework.

I panicked. I looked at Joe, seated next to me, and whispered in his ear. He understood the serious problem I was facing. He held up several of his fingers: that was how much it would cost me. We were friends, but that didn't matter. Business was business.

After I gave him all the coins I had in my pocket, he stood up, looked at the student behind us, and picked up his essay. It was three pages long. Joe copied the best sentences out on a clean sheet of paper, returned the three-page essay to our classmate, and handed me a one-page composition. The only thing I had to do was write my name at the top of the page.

A few days later, when our French teacher returned our compositions to us, along with our grades, I got a 10 out of 10—but the student from whom Joe had borrowed the elaborate write-up got only a 7. The teacher apparently liked my short and concise version. My coins were well spent.

Not too long thereafter, when he was still relatively young, Joe got married, and he asked me to come to his home and have lunch with him and his wife. His apartment was on the first floor of a new building in an exclusive part of Cairo. As soon as I walked in the door, I was amazed by the apartment's size. I knew that neither Joe nor his wife had the means to pay for such a grand residence.

After lunch, Joe and I went for a walk, just the two of us. I asked him how much he was paying in rent. He smiled and said, "Nothing. I own the apartment."

My jaw dropped. "How were you able to afford it?" I asked.

"I bought it for half the list price."

I was speechless.

Joe explained: he had approached the real estate agent and told him that he would buy the model apartment the owners showed their potential tenants. He was willing to pay half price over the course of three years. The real estate agent could continue to show the apartment, but by appointment only. That way, Joe, his wife, and their future baby could live in relative luxury while the owner could collect payments on a space that otherwise would have generated no revenue. "It was a win-win situation," Joe added with a mischievous smile.

In 1956, Eddi, Moti, and I left Egypt, victims of Gamal Abdel Nasser's persecution of the Jews and foreigners living within the nation's borders. But Joe had to remain in Egypt to handle some important businesses. Years later, I got promoted and was in training for my new position at the company's headquarters, in New York City. The company had arranged a temporary apartment for me and my family while we looked for permanent housing. Then a fellow Egyptian immigrant at headquarters told me that Joe had just arrived in the city. He was staying with his wife and son in a modest but nice hotel in a New York suburb.

One weekend, I went out to visit Joe. He was really happy to have gotten out of Egypt when he did. But how, I asked, was he going to live in such an expensive place as New York City?

"Don't worry," he said. "I have plenty of financial resources."

I was curious as to how this could be true. The Egyptian authorities did not allow anyone to leave the country with more than twenty Egyptian pounds.

Joe told me that indeed, he and his wife and son had left Egypt with only twenty Egyptian pounds per person and just a few personal possessions, among which was a small colorful statue of President Nasser depicting him in his bright military uniform dotted with ribbons and medallions. At the Cairo departure terminal, the customs agents asked him why he was taking the statue with him. He told them that he and his family admired Nasser and wanted to keep a memento of all the wonderful years they had spent in Egypt. The customs agents let them through.

"A very risky endeavor with a very lucky outcome," I said. "The Egyptian authorities must have relaxed their restrictions since we left. But what about the American customs?"

When the American agents asked him why he brought the statue with him, he told them that he wanted to have a memento of that SOB Nasser so he could curse it every time he looked at it. Of course, the American customs agents let Joe and his family in without any problem.

By that time, I was dying to see the statue and asked him to show it to me. It was nothing special—a replica of many cheap souvenir statues sold in Egyptian stores and tourist shops.

"Why go to all this trouble to bring it with you?" I asked, puzzled.

"All this *trouble*, my good friend? This is my financial support for the next few years. The statue is made of pure gold!"

The Butterfly

Surgery or no surgery? Sara and I were in disagreement on this issue.

On one side, we had Dr. Chan, a thorough and highly qualified internist who had been taking care of our family for many years. "At your age, with severe atrial fibrillation, your heart may not be able to handle surgery." Dr. Chan was vehemently against the procedure, and he managed to convince Sara and the rest of our family.

On the other side were two well-known orthopedists who specialized in knee replacements. The two operated in tandem: one would replace the left knee while the other replaced the right knee. One of my gym buddies had had a successful double knee replacement performed by these orthopedists. "Why wait until later, when you will be too old to benefit from the surgery?" my friend said. "You better do it now while you're still in good shape."

Both sides had valid arguments. This made my decision even more difficult. But I had to make up my mind—and soon. There was no question that both my knees needed to be replaced.

To help me with the decision, I went to see my electrophysiologist. She was the one who diagnosed my atrial fibrillation. After explaining the situation, I asked her, "Do you think my heart can withstand a double knee replacement?"

"Yes, of course," she answered. "I'll sign the clearance form at any time. Because I don't see your being able to live if you don't exercise. I can't imagine you restricted to a wheelchair or even to a walker. But Avi, why don't you ask the doctors to operate on one knee at a time? The double operation can increase the risk of a heart failure."

I had of course discussed this at length with my orthopedists. Operating on one knee at a time would have required me to go five to six months without exercise. My old muscles would rapidly atrophy.

I told her that I preferred to have both knees done at the same time. If the operation was a success, I'd be a happy fellow. And if my heart succumbed, I'd be happy, too. What better way to die than under anesthesia? Much better than dying while confined to a wheelchair.

The electrophysiologist smiled and said that in the end it was up to me. "I'll text Dr. Chan, and with any luck he will agree with your rationale and respect your decision."

The other choice I had to make concerned the date. I wanted to schedule the operation so that I would be home during Shavuot, the Jewish festival that celebrates the harvest and the revelation of the Ten Commandments at Mount Sinai. During the week of Shavuot, Jews eat mostly dairy products and fruit. But to be honest, I wanted to be home during Shavuot so that I could enjoy the delicious rizogalo that Sara learned to prepare in the Greco-Turkish way from my mother.

Rizogalo is a special rice pudding that my mother used to serve me and my siblings for breakfast daily during Shavuot. She would artfully write our initials in cinnamon on top of the pudding. I was addicted to it. I never wanted the chocolate cake, cheesecake, fruit, hazelnut pie, or anything else she made as much as I wanted that rizogalo.

My operation was scheduled for May 22, just three days before the first evening of Shavuot. Early that morning, Sara took me to the hospital and waited in the reception room while I was being prepared for the operation. The two orthopedic surgeons came to see me and explained the procedure. I didn't pay much attention. I trusted them—in this case with my life.

As soon as I was assigned to a room, I insisted that Sara go home and wait for the nurse to call. I didn't want her to be present if I were to die on the operating table.

After she left, I closed my eyes for a while. When I opened them, I saw two butterflies fluttering their large colorful wings on the window to the left of my bed. I thought, What a pity they can't come in—they are so beautiful.

I closed my eyes again for what seemed to be a fraction of a second. When I opened them once more, I saw the same two butterflies, but this time they inhabited the bodies of two gorgeous women.

One butterfly woman was tall, with light skin, blond hair, and beautiful blue eyes. The other butterfly woman was just as tall, with dark skin, black hair, and beautiful green eyes. Each had a shiny stone embedded in her right palm. The blonde's stone was green; the brunette's was red.

I wondered how the women managed to get into the room. But I didn't have time to ask before the blond butterfly said, "Is your name Avi?" Her voice was smooth and sweet.

"Yes," I answered, amazed.

"We are here to take you to a place where you can rest and relax—an ever-happy place," she explained. They were pulling me out of bed.

I could not resist; it was as if I were hypnotized. They lifted me effortlessly and took me out the window, which opened at our approach. Soon the two butterfly women and I were flying above the trees and buildings outside the hospital.

"My name is Angie," said the blonde with the sweet voice.

"Mine is Azra," said the brunette, whose voice was even sweeter.

They were laughing and singing and occasionally caressed my face.

"Where are you taking me?" I asked.

"To someplace very nice; just wait and see," Angie replied.

"Will my wife and children be there?"

"Your children not yet, but your wife may be soon."

"Is it very far?"

"No," Azra answered. "You see that dark cloud? It's just behind it."

When we came close to the cloud, Azra produced a red stone exactly like the one embedded in her palm and slipped it into my hand. "Don't lose this, Avi. Without it, you cannot cross the dark cloud. You can let it go eventually, but only after you make the crossing." Her voice was a whisper of silk.

Then Angie said, "And this green stone will allow you to get into the garden, your destination. But you cannot let go of it after you enter the garden; it will be embedded in your palm forever."

"Do I have to stay in the garden forever?" I asked.

Angie guessed from my tone that I was anxious. "Yes. But it is a garden where you will be happy and serene. You will never get bored. You'll hear music of all kinds. You'll see nice people young and old, many of whom you've met and known. There are colorful birds and exotic friendly animals there, too." She slipped the green stone into my right hand. "Don't let go of this while crossing the black cloud," she insisted.

"But what if I want to go home?"

"Then you will not be able to get into the ever-happy garden," Angie said.

"And what if I don't want to cross the black cloud?"

"You have to! If you don't, you'll be swallowed by the void and will disappear forever!" Azra warned.

"You're almost there," Angie said, reassuring me. "Just cross the dark cloud and you'll be forever happy."

We stopped high in the air, fluttering our wings to stay in place. Angie and Azra wanted to make sure I would follow their instructions.

I had to decide: Risk being swallowed by the void for a taste of Sara's rizogalo? Or happiness ever after?

"It's Shavuot; I have to be home," I pleaded. "Most important, I can't pass up the rizogalo my wife has prepared for me. She sprinkles my initials in cinnamon on the top."

I was agitated, and while I was fluttering my wings, I lost my grip on one of the stones—I wasn't sure which one. But before I could check and see, a sudden gust of wind formed a dark vortex around me. I was helpless, turning around and around like a basketball spinning on the tip of a finger. I was heading at supersonic speed toward the abyss Azra had warned me about. I closed my eyes, ready to die.

Finally, I stopped spinning and landed with a soft thud. I opened my eyes and found myself lying in bed in my hospital room. I noticed with relief that there were no butterflies at the window.

Someone cautiously opened the door to my room. "He's awake!"

The door opened wide, and a group of people rushed in, some carrying flowers, others carrying potted plants and fruit baskets. My family and other well-wishers had been waiting for me to wake up after the surgery. Sara was holding a large bag.

"What do you have there?" I said.

She smiled and came close to me. "It's your favorite dessert—your beloved rizogalo, with your initials sprinkled in cinnamon. I made it a few days ago," she replied, giving me a hug.

After everyone had left and only Sara remained, her expression turned serious. "What happened?" she asked. "It took you a long time to recover. We were all worried and waited outside your room, talking with your doctors. They assured us that even though such a long recovery time was unusual, you would be okay."

I did not answer, not knowing what to say.

"Were you in pain?" she continued, expecting an answer.

I winked. "Two gorgeous women with very sweet voices wanted to seduce me and take me to an ever-happy garden."

"Oh, I see," she said wryly. "And did you go with them?"

"I told them that I preferred to stay and celebrate Shavuot with you and the children. But really, I just wanted to have my rizogalo."

"Always teasing, Avi. A sign that you are well. The doctors said you'll be discharged tomorrow. We'll be back to take you home."

She leaned over and kissed me. When she stood up, she had a green stone in her hand. It looked very much like the one that Angie, the gorgeous blond butterfly woman, had given me.

"And what is this?" she asked, holding it between her fingers.

"How would I know? Maybe the cleaning woman or one of the nurses brought it in." Somehow, I was able to keep a straight face.

"Should I throw it away?" she asked.

"No. Leave it here with me," I replied casually. Then I added with another wink, "It probably belongs to that gorgeous blond butterfly woman with the beautiful blue eyes and sweet voice." I laughed, and Sara laughed with me.

"You devil," she said, crossing to the door.

My Mother, My Hero

I came back to Tel Aviv after a trip to New York, where I had met with the investment bankers and lawyers who handle our family finances. I had spent the whole week—including the weekend—working to make sure that everything was in order.

It was a fruitful trip, stressful but productive. I picked up my car, which I had left at the airport parking lot, and drove home. It was late, and I just wanted to get to the house, stretch out in my favorite chair, and relax. Sara, I knew, would greet me with her sweet voice and charming smile and wait patiently until I was ready to brief her on the outcome of my New York meetings. Because it was a Monday evening, I knew the house would be quiet and Sara would be relaxed after a weekend full of family activities.

I parked my car in our garage, and as usual I opened the door that led into the kitchen. But the room was unusually dark. I ventured a few steps inside, wondering what was going on, when suddenly the light came on, accompanied by shouts of "Surprise!"

I'd forgotten: it was my birthday.

The kitchen and living room beyond it were full of family and friends, all applauding and coming forward to wish me well. Waiters and waitresses were working their way through the crowd, juggling trays of hors d'oeuvres and glasses of Champagne.

I was happy to see all these people and did my best to thank everyone.

After a while, Sara rang a small handbell to get everyone's attention. She was going to say a few words. She did not like making speeches, so this was indeed a unique and precious gift from her.

After she made a few short but heartfelt remarks, she ended with a traditional Hebrew blessing, "Ad meah ve'esrim" (May he live to be 120). Then she raised her glass and said, "To my husband, Avi, the man with a golden heart."

As soon as she finished, she and I embraced and kissed while the guests applauded. Two waitresses came in carrying a large chocolate cake covered with burning candles.

They placed it in front of us. I was ready to blow out the candles when the guests called out, "Make a wish!" One friend added, "Make the wildest wish you can think of!"

I paused. What was the thing I wanted most? What would be my dream come true? After all, I already had everything my heart desired—a happy and healthy family, good friends, success in my professional life . . . What more was there?

There was no doubt: I wished I had my mother with me.

I closed my eyes and said to myself, I want my mother back. I want to see her one more time. And I blew out the candles.

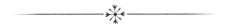

My mother's name was Dora, which means "gold." *She* was the one who had a golden heart; she was gold in everything she did. She smelled like lavender and was never without a smile, even during the hard times—and mostly, they were all hard times because our family was poor.

Despite our precarious financial condition, she managed to take care of her four children—my oldest brother, Arie; my second-oldest brother, Svi; my sister, Dena; and me. She would wake up in the wee hours, clean the house, prepare our breakfast, make sure we had done our homework, and take us to school. She then had to go back home, wash and iron our clothes, and cook—assuming my father had left her some money for groceries, which he wasn't always able to do.

In the afternoons, she hurried to pick us up from school, give us a snack, and watch us while we were doing our homework. And late at night she used to patch our clothes, since we didn't have the luxury of buying new ones. She went to bed after midnight and woke up at five in the morning. Twenty hours of hard work every day.

She helped us with our studies and even devised some homemade toys and games for us to play. During our summer vacations, she would take us to the beach. She inspired us to be honest and stick together as a family.

Above all, she instilled confidence in me at my most vulnerable moments. I was born with a prominent birthmark on my right wrist that was the subject of mockery from my siblings and schoolmates, who teased me about it mercilessly. I used to get into fights trying to stop them, but it only encouraged them to harass me even more.

One day when I was around seven years old, I came home after just such a fight, angry and bleeding. My mother took me on her lap and asked me what happened. I told her that I fell while I was running after the boys who were teasing me. Mom smiled and wrapped her arms around me. I stopped crying, comforted by her lavender scent.

"Avi, my son," she said. "God gave you that birthmark because you're special, because you're smart. Be happy that God has chosen you among all the other boys. You'll see—many good things will happen to you when you grow up."

I raised my head and looked at her.

"You know," my mother continued, "from now on, don't get mad when they tease you. Just tell them that your birthmark is a sign that you've been blessed by God."

I followed my mother's advice, and it worked. My friends' teasing turned into curiosity when I said that my birthmark was a divine gift with mystical powers. I told them that every time I needed help, I just rubbed it and would receive what I asked for, and that's the reason I was getting such good grades in school.

By repeating my story often, I convinced not only my friends but also myself. I thought that my birthmark indeed had miraculous powers and believe that it might even have helped me achieve the happiness and comfort I have today.

My mother died on a sunny Saturday in September, one week before my tenth birthday. She had been in the hospital and was due to come home that day. We had cleaned the house, taken baths, and dressed in our nicest clothes. We were eagerly awaiting her arrival. What we received instead was the devastating news of her death as a result of a pulmonary embolism.

Many images of my mother passed before my eyes. I saw her admiring smile while she watched me on my rocking horse. I saw her stoic smile when, bent over on her low stool, she washed our clothes in a small basin in the kitchen. I saw her resigned smile when she was darning our socks after midnight under a dim light.

But I also saw her beautiful smile on the day when she dressed up and went to see *Romeo and Juliet* starring Norma Shearer and Leslie Howard. She thought that with my curly blond hair and thin face I looked like Leslie Howard.

Yes, I missed her, and I wanted to be with her.

My surprise party was over. The guests had all left. Sara came to me; she was tired and wanted to go to bed. I told her I wanted to remain downstairs just a little longer. She whispered, "Good night, then. Don't stay up too late." Then she kissed me and left.

I was exhausted after my trip New York and even more exhausted after the party. I was half drunk and dizzy from the many glasses of Champagne I had drunk. I just wanted to lie down on the couch in my study and think about my mom.

So I did. I felt as if I were lying on a cloud, floating weightlessly above the room. I was happy and wanted to go upstairs and tell Sara about it. I tried to stand up but fell back on the couch and lapsed into a deep sleep.

When I opened my eyes, I saw a man wearing a white lab coat and two women in blue uniforms staring at me. I was lying in a bed and had wires all over me. There was a tube in my nose, and there were electrodes on my chest and arms. The man and women must have been waiting for me to wake up. They kept looking at the monitors above my bed.

The man in white spoke: "You are in the intensive care unit. Your wife brought you here in an ambulance and explained that in the past you have had vasovagal syncope. She told us she would come back as soon as she gathered a few things you might need."

The doctor added that there was some cause for concern and that he was going to run some tests early in the morning. I was to stay in the hospital a few more days.

He then turned to the two women and said, "This is Aisha, our chief nurse. She's been with us for many years. And this is Lili, who joined us last night. She is an experienced nurse who came highly recommended from a hospital in Norway. She will be taking care of you this evening."

Aisha was an energetic, short woman with African or Middle Eastern features. Lili was a tall, lithe woman with a very prominent bustline.

They left and closed the door behind them. I was frustrated, because I thought the vasovagal condition had been completely cured. But I didn't have much time to think about it, because the door opened, and Lili walked in. She came close to my bed.

"I am an angel," she said. "I was sent here to grant the wish you made at your birthday party."

I laughed. "An angel? You're joking!"

She didn't answer, but she opened her uniform and showed me two large white wings folded across her chest.

I was about to scream, but she put her hand over my mouth. "Shush. If you scream, it will be all over. They will put you in a freezer, then cut you, sew you, and throw you in a hole six feet underground. You don't know where you'll end up. One thing's for sure—you'll never see your mother again."

That got my attention. Then she continued. "Here is the deal: my superiors asked me to offer you two options. You can see your mother and live with her happily ever after, or you can stay a week in heaven, find your mother, spend a few days with her, then apply for an exit visa that will allow you to go back to your family."

She then disconnected all the wires I had on my body, took the blankets off me, and sat on the bed. "We don't have much time, Avi. Hurry up—you need to choose."

This could not be a dream; it was for real. I mean, I could see her doing all these things—fiddling with the wires and blankets, talking, showing me her wings. Lili was an angel for sure, so I knew I had to take her proposal seriously. Staying at the hospital was not an option.

"I would love to live forever with my mother," I said, "but I also want to be with my wife and children. I need them, and they need me."

"It looks like you're better off with the second option, then. However, your return is not guaranteed. Asking for an exit visa involves a lot of paperwork. Most of these requests are turned down, so you risk staying in a separate section where all the people who made such requests are held. You won't be able to stay with your mother for more than just the first few days."

"Am I really dead?" I grumbled.

She smiled. "Very much so."

"If I come back, will I be alive?"

"Yes, you will," she answered.

"I'll take the second option, then. With any luck, I'll be able to get back to my family."

"I'll try to help you," she said, "but it's not a sure thing. Now close your eyes, and we'll be there in a second."

When I opened my eyes, I found myself in front of an austere white building in the middle of a large field of grasses and trees. It looked like it was located at the center of a strange city. There was dense fog as far as the eye could see. Lili was standing by my side. She held my hand and let me take the time to look around.

"What day is it here?" I asked.

"Monday, September eighteenth," she replied. "Our time zone is one day behind yours."

Monday, September 18

"We'll have to get you registered," Lili told me as we entered the stark white building. In the reception area, an old man with long white hair and a white beard rushed toward us. "Hi, Lili," he said. "And you must be Avi. We've been waiting for you."

Lili explained that Emanuel was the best and most knowledgeable counselor around. "We call him Manny. He's a good angel and will take good care of you."

"Are you are going to leave me now?" I asked Lili.

"Don't worry. I'll be watching you and will come back to help if you need me." She gave me a hug and disappeared.

Manny invited me to sit down so he could explain what I needed to know. "This city was created in 1950 because the old city was getting too crowded. It had been overrun by millions of people who had been sent there in the wake of wars, pogroms, the Holocaust, and epidemics. This modern city is divided into neighborhoods that are home to various nationalities. In each neighborhood, the houses are painted a single color. For example, the French houses are white, the British houses are red, the Italian houses are green, and so on. By the way, we have a neighborhood where the houses are a combination of blue, white, and green. It is home to Israeli and Arab soldiers. They live together in harmony. On a Sunday morning, you can watch them playing soccer together."

"What about the terrorists?" I asked.

"Terrorists of any race or religion are in a separate place where you don't want to go." He paused. Then he said, "It's time for your interview with the registrar." He told me that he would be waiting for me when we were finished.

The registrar sat behind a thick glass window. He asked me to sit on a chair that was much lower to the floor than his was. He was a slim man with neatly trimmed black hair, a heavy mustache, and a closely shaved face. He lowered his heavy eyeglasses and looked down at me, taking note of my name, my birth date, the city and country where I was born, and the names of my parents, siblings, and friends.

Then he put down his pen, adjusted his eyeglasses, and said, "You chose the one-week option, which means that at the end of the week you'll be transferred to the place where all those who took that risk and failed are now confined."

"But I hoped I would be able to return to my family," I responded, alarmed.

Without a trace of sympathy, he said, "I can guarantee that you have almost no chance of getting an exit visa. The last person who received one was a German Jew who had won a Nobel Prize and wanted to go back to finalize some of his theories. He claimed they would forever change the world for the better. And that was a century ago! You'd better use your time wisely, because this week is all you get."

I could feel beads of sweat forming on my brow.

He leveled his gaze at me. "So whom do you want to see?"

"My mother, obviously," I responded.

"That is not possible; you can only see her on Friday and Saturday."

I couldn't believe the bombshell he had just thrown at me. "What? Why?"

"Because transportation to the old city has been undergoing major repairs for some time, and it won't be back in working order until Friday."

He reached down into a drawer and handed me a few pills. "Here are seven pills that will help you get through your stay. I always give them to people in situations like this. You need to take one right now."

He waited for me to take it. The pill started working immediately; I felt instantly calmer.

The registrar continued. "On Sunday you must return here to get your papers for the transfer to the other sector. It's the purple sector, but we call it Without Return."

Without Return . . . I didn't like the sound of that. It meant that, in all likelihood, I would never see my family again.

Still, I realized that whatever this place was, it was a place where things could not be changed. Getting mad, screaming, and crying would not help. I had to resign myself to doing the only thing possible under the circumstances: follow the instructions.

I asked, "What should I do during the rest of the week?" I didn't know whether I would be allowed to move around the city. Would I be confined to a house?

He asked whether there were other people I wanted to visit. "You can spend time with whomever you want, but they must have arrived here after 1950."

I thought about this for a moment. Both my parents and two of my siblings had passed on before me. My sister, Dena, was still among the living. So I thought that as long as I was seeing my mother, I might as well take the opportunity to visit with the other members of my family who had crossed over to the other side.

"I would like to visit my father on Tuesday, my eldest brother, Arie, on Wednesday, and my other brother, Svi, on Thursday. I'll spend Friday and Saturday with my mom."

He took note of my requests and prepared passes for me to use. He handed them to me and closed the window. Our conversation was over.

Manny arrived, and together we left the building. As we walked out the door, I happened to glance up. "What are those white birds flying way up high?" I asked.

"Those are not birds," he answered. "They are angels going to or coming back from their assigned missions."

I hoped at least one of them would help me get back to my family at the end of my stay.

"Now I'll take you to your house in the Israeli quarter," Manny told me. "And tomorrow I'll take you to your father."

My house was small but comfortable. It had a bedroom, a bathroom with a toilet and shower, and a kitchenette with a dining table and refrigerator. The living room was furnished with two chairs, a couch, and a TV—which also acted as a phone and a desktop computer. Because I had taken the pill, I was drowsy, and I fell asleep on the couch.

Tuesday, September 19

My father's house was in the Greek quarter. He must have been told of my impending visit, because he was waiting in the doorway for me, wearing the same pajamas he wore when I last saw him in Tel Aviv. He rushed toward me and gave me a long and strong hug.

A blue-and-white sign on his door said TRANSLATOR. I smiled; my father had finally found an easier and more stable occupation than the one he had when we were young. Back then, he was an itinerant fabric salesman. He would carry his wares in a large, heavy suitcase and go to the offices of doctors, bankers, and businessmen to display them. Sometimes he made a sale, but most of the time he didn't.

"Welcome, welcome, my son," my father said in Greek. He ushered me in and asked me to sit on the couch. Then he offered me a Greek coffee—he always got upset when other people called it Turkish coffee.

"So you're a translator now," I said. "Do you like it? Are you happy?"

"Well, I do know a number of languages, and I like to help people who need it. Here, no one gets paid. For me, it's just a worthwhile way to spend my time. And it gives me a certain cachet—I'm important in this neighborhood."

"But are you happy?" I asked again.

He thought for a moment. "This is a nice place. There's never any excitement, but no bad things happen here, either." When I told him I was staying only one week, he didn't say anything. He did not want to ruin the moment.

We talked about many things—sad events, yes, but mostly joyful ones. He brought out his bouzouki, and we sang "To Yelekaki," the song he had played when we lived in Cairo.

"So here in the Greek section, I guess most of your neighbors are Greek, too, yes?" I asked.

Yes, they all were, he said. He and his neighbors would sometimes meet for coffee, or they would get together and have some ouzo, play *tavli* (backgammon), and share some snacks. His friends usually asked him to bring his bouzouki to those gatherings.

"Do you still cook your specialty, arnaki me youvetsi?" This was a delicious lamb-and-orzo stew that he prepared every time Sara and I visited him.

"Yes, I still make it every now and then. I remember how much Sara liked it." Then, as an afterthought, he asked, "Do you still have your Greek passport?"

"I have had many passports because I have lived in several countries," I told him, "but I kept three of them—the American, the Israeli, and the Greek."

He looked at me. "Do you remember what I did to get the Greek passports for you and Sara?"

Of course I remembered, but I didn't answer because I knew he wanted to tell the story again, and I didn't want to deny him that pleasure.

He looked up, as if he were seeing the event in his mind's eye. "As I recall, it was a Friday morning." He smiled. "I went to the Greek consulate in Cairo, and at first I sat patiently in the reception room. The assistant to the consul categorically refused to let me into his boss's office and even stood in front of the closed doors. I was very courteous and tried all the diplomatic techniques at my disposal. He said he wouldn't let me in because I was one of those desperate Egyptians born with no nationality who was trying to get a Greek passport. I begged him, spoke to him in Greek with my Cretan accent, but he thought I was faking it."

He went on, clearly relishing the details. "I sat there another hour or so, but the arrogant bastard wouldn't budge. He acted as if I didn't exist. I couldn't take it anymore. I stood up, insulted his mother and father, pushed him aside, and burst into the consul's office. The consul leaned over in a panic, trying to reach an alarm button on the side of his desk. I raised my hands to show that I was unarmed and did not mean to hurt him. I apologized and explained why I was angry: no one would actually believe I was a Greek citizen. But I was a Cretan, the son of Cretans, and had even fought in the Greek army.

"Then, to prove it, I pulled down my pants, turned around, and showed him the battle scar on my butt. His eyes nearly popped out of his head. Of course, he immediately ordered the assistant to give me whatever I requested."

My dad was happy to relive this event, as always. Afterward, he stood up and said, "Let's have an ouzo." We sat, sipping our drinks, for another hour or more.

Before I left, he stood me in front of his bedroom door, under the mezuzah, and blessed me in a mixture of Greek and Hebrew: "Nahis tin efkimou, pedhimou" (I give you my blessing, my son) and "Yebarechecha Adonai ve yishmerecha" (May God bless you and watch over you).

By that point, Manny was at the door, waiting patiently. It was late, and I had to get back to my temporary home.

Wednesday, September 20

Early the next morning, while I was having tea, Arie called on the all-in-one computer-TV-phone. I was glad to see his face. He hadn't changed much—he still had those devilish eyes behind his thick eyeglasses. "When you come over to my house today, don't be late," he said. "Just kick the door with your foot when you get here."

He was waiting for my expected response. "Why do I have to use my foot?" I asked.

"Because your hands will be full of presents."

He said that many times when we visited him in years past. And we laughed every time. It's not *what* he says, it's the way he says it, Sara always insisted.

Manny rang my doorbell promptly at nine, ready to take me to Arie.

I did not kick the door, and I did not bring any presents, but Arie was happy to see me anyway. He kissed me and poured me a cup of tea. Then he put some crackers and a block of Swiss cheese on the table. "I slipped them into my jacket pocket while I was visiting a neighbor the other night," he explained.

Arie was a hustler and a survivor. In our younger years, he had found ways to make the best out of any circumstance. I remember my mother telling us what he had done when he was just seven or eight years old. His teacher, Madame Shakee, kept him after class because he hit a boy who did not want to share his snack with him. He had to sit still for a solid hour while Madame Shakee sat at her desk reading a book—one eye on the page, the other on Arie.

Arie, of course, wanted to be in the courtyard playing with the other boys. He begged Madame Shakee many times to let him go, assuring her that he would never, ever hit a boy again.

She ignored him and continued reading. In desperation, Arie dug in his pocket and retrieved all the money he had on him, the equivalent of ten cents. He went to her, placed the money on her desk, and said, "Here—take it. Now let me go!"

When Mom arrived to pick Arie up, Madame Shakee told her, "I've been teaching here for more than thirty years, and this is the first time a student has tried to bribe me!" Madame Shakee had a hard time hiding a smile.

Another one of Arie's signature tricks was stealing Svi's only suit on Saturday nights. He would wait until Svi was taking a bath in preparation for going out, then grab the suit, put it on, and wear it to wherever he was going that night.

"That was not nice of me," Arie admitted. "By the way, Svi is doing well now. He is the law enforcement officer in charge of the Israeli quarter here. His house is not far from mine. When you see him, tell him I regret what I did to him when we were young."

I asked Arie how life was in this place. He said that it was better than the life he had had on earth. Nothing was extreme. The nice moments were not so exciting, but the bad moments were fewer and less painful. "It's a peaceful, calm life," he said. "A bit dull, but with no surprises."

He showed me around his house. He had some family pictures on the shelves, and he showed me one of the four of us siblings taken at his bar mitzvah. Pointing to the picture, he said, "Do you remember the day I pushed you off Mrs. Courcou's garden wall? It must have been a year or two before this picture was taken."

How could I forget? It happened on a Saturday afternoon when I was around four years old. My siblings and I and our mother were all gathered at the seven-foot-tall wall that separated the garden belonging to our neighbors—the Courcous—from the street. Mom was talking with Mrs. Courcou, who was leaning out her window. Arie was at her side. I was whining: I wanted to sit on top of the wall. Mom helped me climb up and sat me with my legs hanging down and facing the street. Suddenly, Arie lifted my legs and pushed me over the wall. I fell straight down, headfirst, into Mrs. Courcou's garden and landed only a few inches from the sharp garden tools she kept there. I could have been killed.

"Yes," I said. "I remember very well."

I was carried to my bed and drank a warm Spiro Spathis lemonade that Mrs. Courcou had brought from her house. It was a drink we could not afford to buy.

"After I rested," I reminded Arie, "you came to me, put your arm around me, and handed me your prized flashlight—your beautiful Bakelite flashlight, which nobody was allowed to touch. A nice gesture, for sure—until you took it away again because I was doing better."

We both laughed. I had a nice day with Arie. I was glad he was comfortable and that he seemed calm and relaxed.

On our way home, Manny reminded me that the next morning we were visiting my brother Svi.

Thursday, September 21

Of the four of us, Svi was the quietest. He did not like to talk too much: he didn't get involved in our problems, and he didn't want us to get involved in his. As an adult, he was a man of few words. But those words were usually wise and well chosen.

Svi was always a bit of a dreamer. I remember late one afternoon when we were children, we were all busy doing our homework under Mom's watch. Svi was trying to memorize some Hebrew passages from Genesis about Noah and the flood. The first chapter started with "Noah hatzadik" (Noah was a righteous man). Svi would recite these first few words in a cheerful, loud voice, then close his eyes and fall asleep. Mom tried to help him, but he could not stay awake and concentrate on his lesson. Ever since then, we jokingly referred to him as Noah Hatzadik. He was the first one to laugh about it.

Svi was also the first one in our family to immigrate to Israel. Later on, he became a police superintendent in Tel Aviv. He was given a German shepherd as his partner, and the dog stayed with him all the time, both at work and at home. They made an excellent team.

When Manny dropped me off at Svi's house, Svi greeted me warmly and showed me around. His house was larger than Arie's and Dad's houses. He also had a small garden with fruit trees. Maybe these were privileges that came with his job.

"Did they also give you a dog like the one you had in Israel?" I asked.

He whistled, and a splendid German shepherd came running up and sat at his feet. I inquired about the dog's name. "Irun," Svi answered, then watched my reaction.

Irun was a purebred German shepherd whom Sara and I had gotten when he was only a few weeks old. Sara fed him from a bottle, and he when he got older, he ate food as good as ours—meats, vegetables, rice—as if he were our son. He grew up with our children.

Irun was listening to us, his ears pricked high, his face turned toward me. Did he recognize me? I called him by name. He looked at Svi and then hopped on the couch close to me. I hugged him and kissed him. He began licking my face.

I looked to Svi for an explanation.

"My boss asked me to go to the Dogs section and choose the one I wanted from among the German shepherds," he said. "There were a few of them I liked. When I looked at their records, I recognized the name Irun from all the stories you and Sara used to tell us."

"I'm so glad that you two are together," I told Svi.

"Go on now, Irun. We'll call you when Avi gets ready to leave," Svi told him, and Irun obeyed.

"By the way, do you know whatever happened to the Hawaras?" I asked, referring to the family who used to live in the apartment below ours in Cairo.

"Yes," he replied. "I checked and found out that the three sons are in purgatory. But the mother is here, in a section reserved for Syrian Orthodox women. She was not a bad person, but she could not control her sons."

The building where we lived belonged to a lonely widow who left it after her death to the Syrian Orthodox church. The church allowed Mrs. Hawara and her three sons to move in and live there for free until the sons found jobs. But from the beginning, we sensed the family was not friendly. In fact, they didn't answer the door when we knocked and offered them a tray of sweets as a housewarming gift.

Before daybreak one day, a loud noise shook the floor of our apartment. We all jumped out of our beds, thinking it was an earthquake. As the noise and shaking persisted, we realized that it was coming from the apartment below us. When Dad opened the door to see what was going on, he found an unsigned note lying at our doorstep. It was a warning: we would face even more problems in the future because we were Zionists, enemies of the Egyptian regime.

The knocks on our floor woke us up every night for weeks. It was a nightmare. We tried to talk to the sons, but they refused to come out of their apartment.

I asked Svi if he remembered Hajj Abdou, the owner of the small grocery store located on the ground floor of our building. Yes, Svi remembered him well. Abdou was a widower who lived with his own two big, strong sons. He was also a devout Muslim—honest, courteous, and very kind to everyone our neighborhood. He was universally beloved.

One day Abdou did not show up for work at his store. His absence continued for a very long time; in fact, his sons had to take over the care of the store. When I asked them what happened to their father, they told me that he had been arrested for allegedly belonging to the Muslim Brotherhood, at the time considered a terrorist group.

While in prison, Abdou was tortured and endured long hours of interrogation. He was released, however, after the police found that there was no reason for his arrest in the first place.

Upon his return to work, I went to his store to greet him. He was pale and had lost a lot of weight. He told me in confidence that an investigator revealed that the Hawaras were the ones who had sent an anonymous letter to the secret police accusing him of belonging to the Muslim Brotherhood. I told him about the troubles and frustrations the Hawaras caused us every night. He whispered, "Don't worry, my friend. My sons will take care of them."

The whole thing ended when Abdou's sons started camping out in front of our building, taking turns so that one of them was always there no matter the hour of day or night. They carried large clubs. If one of the Hawaras were to venture out the door, Abdou's sons would beat him and force him back inside. The Hawaras were imprisoned in their apartment.

Finally Mrs. Hawara came down one day, knelt in front of Hajj Abdou's sons, and cried. They were starving, and she wanted to be allowed to go out and buy food. She admitted that her sons were good-for-nothing bums. They refused to find jobs and relied on church charities to survive.

Two days later, the church evicted them from the apartment. And that is how the whole ordeal ended.

"Good riddance," Svi said. "At least they didn't cause us any physical harm."

We both took a deep breath and brought up many other memories of our years together.

When it was time for me to leave, Svi called for Irun, who hopped up on the couch and kissed me again. I kissed him goodbye in return.

Manny was at the door. "Please tell your brother that you may need his help when it comes time to ask for your exit visa," he suggested. "Maybe he knows some big shot who could pull a few strings."

When I brought up the subject, Svi shook his head. "I'm afraid I can't help," he said. "Unfortunately, the registrar has absolute authority on these matters."

Friday, September 22–Saturday, September 23

When I got back to my house Thursday evening, I discovered that my mom had left me a text message on my all-in-one computer-TV-phone. She asked me to have Manny take me to the school adjacent to her house early the following morning. She wanted me to be present while she was teaching. "Just come in and sit at the back of the classroom," she said.

On Friday morning, the class was full of children, but there were also some men and women—old and young, of many races—in the room as well. When my mother saw me making my way to the last row, she stopped and gestured toward me. "This is my dear son Avi, whom I've talked so much about," she said to the class.

Then she rushed to me and took me in her arms. She had the same scent of lavender that had been so reassuring and comforting when I was a kid. We kept hugging for a long time. The students stood up and applauded.

"Stay here for the rest of the class, Avi. I'm sure you'll enjoy it."

She went back to the front of the class and continued her teaching. I did not pay much attention because I felt tipsy with emotion. I didn't want to lose the feeling—I wanted to experience the sensation of being in her arms forever.

I don't know how long it was before my mother raised her voice and called my name. "Avi," she said, "it's time to tell the class a couple of stories, as I used to do when I helped you with your studies. I'm going to tell the first one, about cheating, and then I'm going to ask you to tell the second one, about solidarity."

My mother stood up and started walking around the students' desks. "When I was a young girl, I attended a French school," she said. "I learned that in French, the Red Sea is called la mer Rouge. The English Channel is called la Manche. And 'manche' is also the French word for 'sleeve.'

"During Passover, our teacher wanted us to recite some biblical passages in French about the Jewish exodus from Egypt. She also asked questions related to the texts we recited. When the first student came to the front of the room, she recited the passage about Moses making a pathway through a big body of water so the Jews could escape the pursuing Egyptians.

"'And what is the name of the sea that Moses parted?' the teacher asked.

"The student did not know the answer. Seeking help, she glanced at a friend seated in the front row. This girl was wearing a bright red dress with long sleeves. Trying to help, her friend pointed her finger to her red sleeve—thinking that its red color would be the perfect prompt.

"Relieved, the student standing in front of the class answered in a loud and confident voice, 'La Manche.'

"She only realized her mistake when the whole class burst into laughter."

Then it was my turn to tell a story. My mother handed me a few sticks and said, "Go ahead."

I stood up and began. "My mother raised four children, three boys and one girl. We played together and got along very well, except sometimes we had our differences. One day, after she had to intervene in one of our skirmishes, she asked us to sit around our kitchen table. She had something important she wanted to tell us. It was about the benefits of solidarity among family members, especially siblings.

"She lined up five sticks on the table in front of us," I continued.

Then I also lined up five sticks on the desk of a student sitting in front of me. I told him, "Pick up one stick and break it."

He did so with ease.

"And now pick up the remaining four sticks, hold them together, and try to break them," I instructed. He tried and tried, but he could not do it.

"That's exactly what our mom wanted to teach us," I explained. "Her influence inspired the four of us to remain united under all circumstances. Never again did anything come between us. I hope this demonstration will have the same effect on all of you." Afterward, the students crowded around us to thank me and my mother.

When all the students had left, my mom turned off the light, and we walked arm in arm through the school's back door and out into the sunset. We took a short stroll and entered her house through the kitchen.

Her house was the same size as my dad's and Arie's but smaller than Svi's. However, it was better organized, fresher, and smelled nicer. The scent of flowers and fruits arranged in the living room blended with the aromas of food and spices emanating from her kitchen. We sat in the living room and began to chat.

We talked about my childhood, about our lives in Egypt and afterward. She wanted to know where we lived and what we did. She also asked about our children and grandchildren. Then she posed and took my hand. "How is Dena, my one and only daughter?"

I told her that Dena was devastated by the loss of her mother, as we all had been. But soon after, Dena had assumed the role of the woman of the house and took care of us. "She lives in Tel Aviv with her children, grandchildren, and great-grandchildren now," I added.

My mother smiled and said, "I knew she could take care of the house—and that she would be especially good with you and your brothers."

I asked my mother about her life in this new place. She said that in the beginning she was bored because there wasn't much to do except clean the house. Then she got approval to open the school. And over time she met other women from Greece, Turkey, and the Middle East. "We each bring some food typical of our countries to our meetings. If you come, you'll enjoy all kinds of delicacies and hear all the languages from that part of the world, including Hebrew, Greek, Arabic, Turkish, Armenian, and Ladino."

She placed a tray of nuts and fruits in front of me. She said she had to go to the kitchen and heat our Shabbat dinner. "I prepared everything yesterday, so it will be ready very soon."

I felt calm in this serene house. I sipped chilled rose water from a tall glass my mom had placed on the table and picked at some nuts. I also tasted the delicious dried figs she had laid out, just like the ones Dad used to claim were from Smyrna—the ones we had on the rare occasions when he had a good day selling his fabrics.

My mother came back with a candle, a piece of challah, and a small bottle of red wine. She handed me a yarmulke and said, "Let's say our Shabbat evening blessings." She covered her head with a scarf, then we blessed the candle's light, the fruit of the vine, and the bread.

"Shabbat shalom," she said as she kissed me. "Now please go and take these nuts and fruits back to the kitchen while I bring our dinner to the living room."

Then we sat down and ate what I thought was the most delightful food I've ever had.

Afterward, we slept in her bed, where I embraced her as I had when I was a child. In the morning, we went back to the school, which also served as a synagogue, and attended Saturday services.

Late that afternoon, we enjoyed another lavish dinner, including a Greek salad, barbounia (red mullet), dolmades (stuffed grape leaves), bourekas (dough stuffed with cheese), loukoum (Turkish delight), and basboussa (semolina cake with syrup). In the center of the table, Mom had placed a large bowl of rice pudding—her famous rizogalo, with a calligraphic *A* dusted in cinnamon on top. "I remember how much you like rice pudding," she said, watching me devour it.

Before I left, Mom went into her bedroom and came back carrying a wooden box. When she opened it, I saw that there was a mirror on the inside of the lid. "A very kind and famous inventor offered it to me when he saw what I was doing at the school," she said. "He asked me if I had family members who were still on earth, and I said yes. He offered me this box and said, 'Now you can see them whenever you want.' Take it—I'm sure I can get another one from him. I hope it will allow you to see me, too." She wrapped the box in red paper and handed it to me. I took it and held it as if it were a precious jewel.

"How was your stay with your mom?" asked Manny on our way home that night.

"Divine," I answered. "It was worth it, even if it means I'll have to spend my remaining time in the Without Return sector."

"I'm glad, because the exit visa is impossible to obtain. In any case, you must see the registrar tomorrow morning to get transferred to your new home."

His words brought me crashing back down to reality. I entered my house, took a pill, and dropped onto my bed.

Sunday, September 24

When I opened my front door on Sunday morning, I was very surprised to see Lili standing there with Manny. She was holding a large brown envelope.

"Hurry up," she ordered. "We need to go pick up your brother Svi. I called him, and he's waiting for us."

When we arrived at his house, Svi was outside. Lili opened the envelope and showed him its contents. Svi nodded and said, "I'm coming with you."

Inside the stark white building, the reception room was empty, probably because it was Sunday—or maybe because my case was the only one scheduled that day. But behind his thick glass window, there was the registrar, sporting a sadistic smile.

The four of us approached the window. The registrar wiped a few drops of coffee from his mustache, lowered his eyeglasses, and said, "Pay close attention to all the instructions I'm going to give you now. Then I will hand you the documents you need to proceed to the Without Return sector." He was ready to start his long monologue when Lili passed the big brown envelope to him through the slot at the bottom of the window. We stood still, waiting for his reaction.

He hastily looked at the contents of the envelope, then turned a ghostly white. "Who gave you these?" he demanded. "And what do you want?"

Lili leaned closer to the window and said evenly, "Who gave them to us? One of your disgruntled assistants, of course. And what do we want? We want you to give the exit visa to Avi right now. If you don't, this police officer"—she pointed to Svi—"will immediately take you to your superiors."

The registrar looked around to make sure the room was still empty. Without saying another word, he took an ink pad and a set of stamps out of his desk drawer and, with a shaking hand, stamped the exit visa authorization on a piece of paper.

Lili took it, examined it, and turned to us. "We are ready to go now," she said.

"Where?" I asked.

"Back to the place I took you from. Remember to close your eyes during our trip."

"Wait!" I said. "What was in the envelope?"

With an amused look, she said, "Let's just say that he and Merlyn, his secretary, were caught in some compromising positions."

"Merlyn," I repeated. "Don't tell me it was . . . Merlyn Monroe!"

She nodded. "If you have any other questions, you better ask them now," said Lili.

I took a moment to think. Suddenly I remembered that I needed an answer to a question that had obsessed me ever since I joined the firm that I worked for for so many years. I turned to Lili and asked, "Do you know whether there is a Jefferson Julien Pachebat III here?"

"Yes. His house is not far from this building. Do you really need to see him?" asked Lili, hoping I would say no.

"Yes, I do. I have a question that only he can answer."

"We'd better hurry, then."

I bade both Svi and Manny goodbye and thanked them for their hospitality. I was ready to see Jeff Pachebat.

Jeff Pachebat was the man who had hired me at the company where I built my career. He hired me even though I couldn't speak English and had no experience in the company's industry. To say that I remain grateful to him is an understatement.

Soon Lili and I arrived in a neighborhood where the houses were all painted yellow. "This section is reserved for business celebrities," Lili said in a respectful tone.

I looked around and found a house with Jeff's name engraved on a copper sign. Below it were the words CHAIRMAN OF THE IMPROVEMENT COMMITTEE. That didn't surprise me at all.

Jeff opened the door. "Avi!" he yelled, pulling me into a hug with his strong arms. "What are you doing here?" I described the events preceding my arrival. "It's good you're going home. It's nice here, but there's no action. Things move slowly, and life here is too sedentary for you."

We sat down and had coffee together. He asked about Sara and our daughters, whom he knew from the many years we spent together. I asked him what he was up to. "I'm the chairman of the improvement committee," he said. "Right now I'm trying to submit a proposal to improve the traffic system. Some of the equipment is old and causes serious delays, like the one we had a few days ago." I nodded. That was the reason I could not visit my mother when I first arrived.

Jeff had been the chairman and CEO of our company before he retired and moved to Florida. But then his health began to decline, and he was moved into a memory-care facility soon after he was diagnosed with Alzheimer's disease. He had died at the age of ninety-seven.

Jeff had been my mentor during my first and most critical years at the company. He watched me pursue the same career path he had and was very proud of my success. So I was glad to see that he did not show any signs of dementia here. I realized that one must die to get rid of this horrible disease.

"Jeff," I said, "I want to ask you a question that I did not have the opportunity to ask—or, to be frank, did not dare ask—when we worked together."

"And what is this burning question?"

"When you interviewed me for the job, I could not speak English, and I had no experience in the company's industry. Why did you hire me?"

Jeff put his hand on my shoulder and looked at me with the mischievous smile that usually preceded one of his biting remarks.

"Avi, everyone makes mistakes."

This was the Jeff I missed and admired. This was the Jeff who pulled me and pushed me when I needed it. He knew when and how to use wit. He was my mentor, the best and kindest in the whole world.

I laughed, but I didn't pursue the question further. I needed to get going.

On my way out, Jeff held me in front of him with both hands and looked straight into my eyes. "Avi, I hired you because I saw in you the hardworking and determined young man I was at your age."

I had tears in my eyes when I left.

An impatient Lili was waiting outside Jeff's front door.

"Close your eyes," she said. "When you open them again, you'll be in the same room and in the same bed you were in when we left. It will still be Monday evening, September eighteenth."

I suddenly realized that something was missing. "Where is the box my mother gave me?" I asked.

"What box?" Lili replied.

I was back in my hospital bed. Lili was standing in front of me, the way she had been before our journey. This time, however, she did not wear her nurse's uniform. She just waved her wings and said, "Enjoy your family and friends. I hope to see you when it's your time. And be careful what you wish for—you just might get it!"

Then she spread her wings and disappeared.

In the morning, two nurses came in and took me for the tests the doctor had ordered. Then they brought me back to my room in time for breakfast. I anxiously awaited the doctor's visit and the results of the tests.

He came in while I was watching TV. He sat down and got straight to the point. "All the results came in: you're as fit as a fiddle. Aisha called your wife and gave her the good news. She's coming soon." Aisha arrived to help me get ready.

What a wonderful adventure I went through, I thought. True, the registrar was a mean old coot who only wanted to see me anxious and sad. But what a pleasure it was to spend time with my dad and my two brothers. And what a magical couple of days I had with my mom, my hero. I just was sorry to have lost the box she gave me. Still, as my mother used to say in French, "Tout est bien qui finit bien" (All's well that ends well).

Sara arrived to take me home. That evening, she said, "Now that we know you're in good health, you'll have to write thank-you notes to everyone who sent you gifts while you were in the hospital. I've taken them out of their packaging and arranged them on our dining table next to the names and addresses of the people who sent them."

She was ready to leave my study, but she stopped. "There is one gift that had no card attached, so I don't know who sent it. It's an empty wooden box with a mirror under the lid—unremarkable except for the beautiful red paper it was wrapped in. If you don't need it, I can use it."

"No," I said. "I think I know who sent it. I'll keep it in my study. It's from a friend who's known me since I was a baby." I smiled and took Sara in my arms.

"Life is beautiful," she said, taking the words right out of my mouth.

The Woke Rabbi

Rabbi Ben Kahn was the youngest rabbi ever to officiate at Congregation Emet Shalom, located in one of the wealthiest suburbs in New Jersey. As a matter of fact, he may well have been the youngest rabbi in the United States—maybe even in the whole world. He was only twenty-four years old.

His mother, born in Morocco, was a teacher at the Paris Opera Ballet School. His father was born in Germany and was a well-known orchestra conductor. They met during a gala sponsored by the American Jewish Federation, then got married and settled in New York.

Having a child was not part of Ben's parents' plans. They intended to pursue their artistic lives to the fullest. But God had other plans, and Ben was conceived after a sumptuous dinner his parents had attended in Vienna.

Ben was a good student, possessing way-above-average intelligence. He was considered a genius by his schoolmates. He was not, however, a bookworm. He loved sports and was the best baseball player at his high school. He also liked to paint, and all signs indicated that painting was to be his career.

During his senior year of high school, he attended a service at a synagogue in Brooklyn with his parents. The old rabbi gave a sermon full of Hebrew citations from the Torah and other religious books. Most of the congregants found it difficult to follow.

Ben, raised by devout Jewish parents, was a firm believer in God and the Torah. Like his parents, he respected and followed Jewish laws and traditions. But the old rabbi's sermon that day was boring. It drove the few young people in attendance to go out for "fresh air." The old-fashioned rabbi was in part the reason why the number of young congregants at the synagogue was dwindling.

Ben was thinking that things could be different—more exciting, more interesting, more engaging . . . more *modern*. That same night, Ben told his parents he wanted to become a rabbi.

He got his master's degree in theological studies, then was ordained at a rabbinical seminary. He spent a year as an assistant rabbi in a New York synagogue. But in his heart, he knew he was destined for greater things.

The opportunity arose when the rabbi of Emet Shalom died on the operating table during open-heart surgery.

Although Ben was ashamed to admit it, he was overjoyed when he heard about the rabbi's death. Emet Shalom was the wealthiest congregation in the country. Many deep-pocketed Jewish families traditionally provided the necessary funds for its most ambitious projects. In fact, there was a rivalry among the richest Jewish families in New Jersey and even in New York as to who could contribute the most money to its coffers. Emet Shalom, of course, was happy to fan the flames of such a competition.

To encourage the largest possible donations, the synagogue offered members numerous opportunities to have their names prominently displayed on its buildings and grounds. It seemed that there wasn't any structure, fixture, or part of the property that couldn't be named.

Ben knew there were many rabbis more experienced than he was who would apply for the job at Emet Shalom. But he wanted to try his luck, confident that if he could get an interview with the synagogue's board, he would come out on top. And indeed, Ben charmed his interviewers with his ideas, enthusiasm, determination, and maturity. They voted to hire him unanimously.

Ben's first year as rabbi of Emet Shalom was an immense success. He organized a middle-school baseball tournament. He directed and participated in plays during Purim and Hanukkah. He played golf and poker with the older members.

The number of young congregants increased noticeably. Everyone, young and old, loved Ben, and he loved his job. He was proud of his leadership and felt confident that he could start implementing some of the modern reforms he had in mind.

One of his most daring suggestions was to stop the practice of displaying the names of donors in the synagogue. Instead, he wanted to name projects and structures after religious concepts such as love, harmony, and hope. He wanted all donations to be anonymous so that everyone could share ownership of the synagogue. He was confident that this would create an inspirational model for other congregations worldwide.

He presented his plan to the board of directors, who at the beginning showed skepticism and even concern. In the end, however, they succumbed to Ben's determination and enthusiasm.

Rosh Hashanah was approaching, and Ben thought it was an ideal opportunity to announce the new policy. He was going to do it as part of the sermon he was to deliver on the first night of Rosh Hashanah so that the practice could start at the beginning of the new year. The sermon would focus on the theme of donations and charity. He spent many late nights reading the Torah, the Midrash, the Talmud, and various religious and scholarly texts. He revised the sermon many times. When he rehearsed it in front of his bedroom mirror, he smiled: he knew he had a poignant and convincing message to deliver.

On the first night of Rosh Hashanah, a solemn and reverent atmosphere prevailed in the sanctuary. The richest benefactors were present with their families and were seated in the front rows. Ben stood alone on the bimah, dressed in an immaculate white robe and a large white-and-blue tallit that covered almost all of his body. It was time to deliver his sermon.

He spoke in a vigorous and passionate voice, telling his listeners that the only good deeds were those done anonymously. He cited many examples from the Jewish, Christian, and Muslim scriptures that emphasized the importance of anonymity when making donations of any kind.

He cited Maimonides's eight levels of charity, the second, third, and fourth of which describe the value of giving anonymously. He also cited a passage from the New Testament book of Matthew: "Therefore when thou doest thine alms, do not sound a trumpet before thee." He ended his sermon by paraphrasing the eighteenth-century English historian William Hutton: "The charity that hastens to proclaim its good deeds is only pride and ostentation."

His sermon was passionate, vigorous, and heart-wrenching at the same time. Standing with his arms held toward the sky, he looked like a fervent prophet. Light shining down on him from the large chandelier above his head only reinforced that impression. The audience was fascinated. Some congregants even applauded, a demonstration usually forbidden in synagogues during services.

Rabbi Ben went home that evening happy and proud of himself. It seemed as if it wasn't going to be so hard to make changes after all.

A few days later, he ordered all the exterior and interior walls to be repainted and refinished so that no one could see the names of the people who had made donations. Plaques inscribed with donor names were to be removed. Ben was finally realizing his dream.

Four months after Rosh Hashanah, northern New Jersey was hit by a tornado that leveled several communities. Emet Shalom wasn't as heavily damaged as some buildings, but a considerable amount of money was required to replace its air-conditioning and heating system. In addition, Ben wanted to take the opportunity to build a playground and a basketball court as part of the reconstruction. He knew the wealthy families would respond generously, as usual.

A few weeks later, though, when he spoke with the synagogue's treasurer, he was surprised by the insignificant amount of money that had been donated, the sum totaling only a few hundred dollars—nothing compared to the millions Emet Shalom used to get under such circumstances.

Months passed by, but no major donations were forthcoming. Finally the board of directors invited the rabbi to an extraordinary meeting in which they told him that he was released from his position. They were under pressure from wealthy members to let him go. They wished him good luck in his next job.

Ben was sad that evening. He continued to believe that his approach to giving was the right one—God had made that perfectly clear. The board of directors and the wealthy congregants were wrong.

The next morning, he prepared his breakfast, smiled in the mirror, and said with a sigh, "Screw it. I'm going back to painting."

Longevity

At sixty-five, I'd retired from the multinational corporation where I'd spent more than forty years. During that time, I had acquired the reputation of being Mr. Fix-It, not only within our company but also among Wall Street banks and asset management firms.

It was no surprise, then, when a few months into my retirement, several companies that were in bankruptcy or about to file for it sought out my services. The most challenging was a publicly owned construction company that was the industry leader in its line of products. The company had expanded through the acquisitions of smaller companies but got into serious trouble when it took over its main competitor.

I was brought in as CEO, and thanks to a skillful finance director and a young managerial team, we succeeded in turning the company around. After two years, we were ready to contact the Wall Street firms that had been shying away from us in the past. We wanted them to invest in our company, and we wanted their financial analysts to rate our company's stocks as a strong buy.

Don, my finance director, and I took a one-week tour of the most important asset management firms in the country, most of which were located in New York City. That Friday morning, we had one more investment firm to visit before ending our tour.

It was a very large, important firm run by a woman known as the Dragon Lady. She was in her midfifties and had a reputation for extreme toughness. In addition, she was a fitness freak—a Pilates adept who ran five miles every morning before work.

The Dragon Lady received us in her immense office. She was sitting at the head of a long table, and there were twelve executives sitting around her, all wearing dark suits and white shirts. After the customary greetings, Don and I got ready for what we called the Don and Avi Show.

Because we were addressing an audience we'd never met before, I decided to tell a story that one of my bosses had used to warm up audiences whenever he gave a speech. It was a good way to break the ice. While Don was setting up the equipment for our slide presentation, I stood at the opposite end of the table, facing the Dragon Lady.

I explained that our presentation would last only twenty minutes. I mentioned that it was comprehensive and covered all areas of our operations. I said that at the end there would be ample time for the audience to ask questions. Then, looking at the Dragon Lady, I added, "I'll do my best to address them, but please don't get mad if the answers aren't what you expect." Then I said that I wanted to tell them a story about a lion. It went something like this:

> A young lion wanted to make sure that all the jungle inhabitants recognized him as the king of the jungle. He found a monkey, grabbed him by his neck, and asked him, "Who is the king of the jungle?"
>
> "You are," answered the trembling monkey.

The lion then jumped on the back of a giraffe. "Who is the king of the jungle?" asked the lion with a loud roar.

"You are," answered the giraffe, who could feel the lion's fangs ready to sink into his flesh.

The lion repeated the same maneuver with every animal he encountered. When he arrived in front of his den, he put his forelegs on a rock and with his loudest roar announced to all the animals that he was the king of the jungle. But at that moment, he saw an elephant walking nonchalantly a few yards away, minding his own business. The lion could not let this creature remain so indifferent. He ran around the elephant and roared many times, asking, "Who is the king of the jungle?" But the elephant just kept walking, ignoring the lion's presence and his roars.

Frustrated, the angry lion then jumped on the elephant's back, put his head in the elephant's ear, and roared, "Who is the king of the jungle?"

The elephant had had enough. He grabbed the lion with his trunk and threw him to the ground. The lion couldn't move. He was covered with dirt, all four legs in the air.

Subdued, the lion looked up at the elephant and said, "You don't have to get so mad if you don't know the answer."

There was loud laughter from the executives around the table, but it was cut short when they saw that the Dragon Lady reacted with just a grin and a look at her wristwatch.

Our slide presentation showed a very convincing picture of the improvements we had made at our company. It also emphasized the solid foundation we had built for continuous and sustainable growth. At the end, I wrapped up with my preferred closing sentence: "As you saw in the graphs, all the lines that should go up are up, and all the lines that should go down are down."

Then we were ready for questions. All the executives turned to the Dragon Lady, waiting for her reaction.

She paused, her chin resting in her hand. Then, pointing at me, she asked, "How old are you?"

"Around seventy," I answered.

"How old are your siblings?"

"In their eighties. I'm the baby, and we are all very healthy and fit."

She continued to ask questions about my age, my family's health, and my fitness. I told her that I exercised every day and mentioned the races I'd run, including the tough Boston marathon.

At that point, Don, who was surprised and somewhat irritated by all those questions, looked at the Dragon Lady and said, "We had a push-up competition at the office, and Avi did twice as many as the young guys did."

That didn't seem to make a difference to the Dragon Lady. "What medicines are you taking? Can you write them down for me?"

I tore off a piece paper from a legal pad in front of me. I looked at Don, who was about to scream, and calmed him down with a wink. Then I wrote on the piece of paper, folded it, and asked one of the executives to pass it to the Dragon Lady.

The entire group was waiting for her reaction. Then she emitted a loud burst of laughter.

She turned the piece of paper around and showed the group what I had written in very large letters: NO MEDICINE, NOT EVEN VIAGRA!

She mentioned in a relaxed and friendly tone that she was very impressed with our success story. Then, addressing one of her executives, she ordered him to immediately acquire a significant amount of our shares.

"And now it's time for lunch," she said. "Won't you join us? We have plenty of sandwiches and salads." Don and I accepted the invitation.

When we were finished eating, I told the Dragon Lady that we had to leave. She and her executives were just then tackling the dessert table, filled with chocolate cookies and brownies.

"Why so early? To another presentation?" she asked, a brownie in her hand.

"No, no more presentations—we're going home."

"Oh, I see. At your age it's good to take the afternoon off and rest."

That last remark triggered an impulse to repay the Dragon Lady for all her indiscreet questions. I thought of a funny story a friend of mine from the gym had emailed to me.

"No, no rest, either. My wife and are attending the wedding of my uncle Shmuel."

"Your uncle?" the Dragon Lady looked at me with bewilderment. "How old is your uncle?"

"He is ninety-three," I responded casually.

"Gosh, why marry at that age?" she asked.

"He doesn't want to—it's his mother who's pushing him," I answered. We all laughed.

The Dragon Lady shook my hand with a smile—she probably understood the reason I told the story.

When we reached the elevator, Don gave me a high five, a gesture he always used after exceptionally successful events.

The Good Neighbors

One day, when Sara and I were living in a suburb of New York City, new neighbors, a family of five, moved into the house next door to ours.

The house was previously owned by an old couple who decided it was time to spend their remaining years in assisted living. But unlike the old couple, who preferred to be alone rather than mingle with their neighbors, the new family was young, energetic, and outgoing.

The first Sunday after they moved in, the husband knocked on our door to introduce himself. I invited him in, and we sat down in the living room to chat. Matteo de Luca, his wife, Monica, and their three boys had just come from an apartment in the Bronx. They decided to move to the suburbs because they wanted a larger and quieter place. Even though the quality of the public schools in our neighborhood was high, Matteo explained, he and Monica sent their boys to boarding school, where they would be safe while their parents made increasingly frequent trips to visit relatives in Sicily.

Matteo was the owner of Franklin Electrical Sales and Service, a company founded by his father. Among the many things he shared with me was how much he appreciated Italian wines, which his father had introduced him to. I immediately went to my wine fridge and opened a bottle of Chianti. Matteo tasted it and gave it a thumbs-up.

After we had drunk a couple of glasses, he mentioned that he was planning to leave an extra set of keys to his house with me, just in case something happened during one of the family's trips to Sicily.

It didn't take long for Monica, too, to visit and establish a good relationship with Sara. Monica was an ebullient and joyful woman, always ready to help. She and Matteo invited us to birthday and anniversary celebrations, and we reciprocated in kind. We became friends.

The de Lucas' home was a one-story house with a very large backyard, separated from ours by a wooden fence, where they installed a nice swimming pool and a basketball court. They also improved the landscaping by adding ornamental plants, mature trees, and colorful flowers and shrubs. Because Sara and I lived in a two-story house, we could see the de Lucas' backyard from one of our upstairs windows and enjoyed watching what the neighbors were up to. During the summers, the boys' joyful screams and laughter echoed in our house.

Matteo was a skillful handyman. He fixed our electrical appliances and performed many other household tasks for us. Sara was happy to rely on someone who could take care of bothersome issues when I was too busy to handle them. Our families got together often—Monica and Sara would prepare a variety of Italian and Middle Eastern dishes, and Matteo and I would select a good Italian wine. We saw each other almost daily on the doorsteps of our homes, too. We were delighted to have such good neighbors.

But after a couple of years, the visits suddenly stopped. We didn't give it much thought, assuming that the de Lucas might be traveling more than usual or were dealing with some private family matter.

One night, Sara, who couldn't sleep after watching a few episodes of *Murder, She Wrote*, got out of bed and went to the guest room across the hall. She opened the window to get some fresh air and casually looked out at the de Lucas' backyard, where she saw a shadow wearing a black nightgown dragging a dark plastic bag close to an area that was mounded with earth.

What could that be?

She rushed back to the bedroom and woke me up.

"Avi, some weird things are going on in the de Lucas' backyard," she said, her voice shaking.

I followed Sara sleepily across the hall. I looked through the window but saw nothing unusual—no shadows, no plastic bags. All dark and quiet. Sara nudged me aside and spent a long time scrutinizing the backyard, but everything seemed normal.

When we returned to the bedroom, Sara was swearing on her father's grave and on every other sacred thing that she saw a shadow dragging a plastic bag across the yard.

"I have a busy day tomorrow," I said, a trace of impatience in my voice. "Let's go to sleep now, and over breakfast, we'll talk about what you saw."

Sara acquiesced and got into bed, pulling the blanket up to her chin. But she whispered, "I think she killed him and buried him."

Over the course of the following days, with clearer heads, Sara and I discussed what could possibly have happened. Killing someone and burying him in his own backyard was a very risky feat, nearly impossible nowadays. Besides, there were other more likely reasons for the de Lucas' absence—a long trip, a divorce, a stay in rehab . . . maybe troubles with the IRS.

Still, I noted that Matteo never did drop off the keys to his house as he said he would. Did he change his mind? I even stopped by Matteo's office to ask whether everything was all right, but his staff didn't know where he was.

After a while, we stopped wondering what happened. After all, if the de Lucas needed help, or if they wanted us to know what was going on, they would have said something. So we respected their wishes.

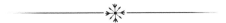

A few years passed, and Sara and I reached the occasion of our fiftieth anniversary. We decided to spend it at a resort in Bali, on a second honeymoon.

On our last day, we were lying on the resort's white sand beach, catching a few final rays of sun. It was early afternoon, and the beach was almost deserted.

But not very far away, there was a couple hugging, kissing, and laughing. Sara turned her head and looked at them; she thought she recognized the woman's laughter. "I think the woman with that man is Monica," she said to me under her breath. I looked at them, certain that Sara was imagining things, and went back reading my book.

But Sara sat up on the straw mattress and faced me. "It's Monica," she hissed. "Look at her—she's standing now, almost naked in her bikini. She's with another man!"

I looked again. "It *might* be Monica," I said, "but then again it might not."

That evening over dinner, we didn't talk about Monica or Matteo. We did not want to spoil our last night in Bali.

On the plane early the next morning, Sara looked at me and said, cup of coffee in hand, "*Now* do you believe me that she killed him and buried him in their backyard?"

The Lost Island

One year, I asked Sara what she wanted most for her birthday.

She didn't answer at the time, but she had always loved to travel, and she and I had been to a number of popular destinations on many continents over the years. She knew she wanted to go on a trip, but she asked me for some time to think about it—she wanted to research the possibilities and choose a place we'd never been to before. "We've had many enjoyable visits to cities far and wide," she said. "But we've always been part of a well-organized cruise or tour group. Let's be more adventurous this time, while we're still able to do it." Of course, I agreed without hesitation.

Sara conducted a meticulous, intensive search. And after several days, she came up with a plan to visit an island in the Gulf of Thailand normally not included in commercial tours or cruise itineraries. It was Koh Rong, off the southern coast of Cambodia. "Like the James Bond island that was little known before the movie," Sara explained, leafing through the pages of an atlas.

We had decided that the most efficient way to organize our trip was to fly to Bangkok and from there to Koh Rong. But Thai Airways had only one flight per day from Bangkok to the island. And when we arrived at Bangkok, we had to wait at the airport because the flight to Koh Rong was delayed by weather conditions. The delay lasted several hours—so long that many passengers canceled their trips. Sara and I, however, together with eight other die-hard passengers, decided to wait.

Late at night, we boarded the Airbus. It was extremely strange to walk onto a plane in which there were around ninety empty seats. The group spread out—some sat in front, others sat in the middle, and Sara and I decided to sit in the back.

Sara liked to give imaginary names to strangers based on their appearance. She said it helped her remember them, and it gave her a quick way to refer to them in conversation. She discreetly pointed to a young couple sitting in the front row, both wearing thick eyeglasses. These two she called the Nerds. She thought they were probably on a mission to discover new species of plants and animals.

She guessed that the old couple sitting in the middle of the plane were Jews from Brooklyn. They were both short and thin but lively and energetic. These people she named Mr. and Mrs. Borshdbelt. According to Sara, they had probably chosen this challenging adventure as their last hurrah before giving up traveling altogether.

Sara looked at a man sitting a few rows behind the Borshdbelts and surmised that he was a retired American military officer. He was in his midfifties and still in great shape. Sara named him Mr. Commando—probably a former Green Beret, she decided.e was He

And finally, there were three Thai or Cambodian young men sitting a few rows in front of us. They wore blue coveralls and acted as if they wanted to be left alone. Sara called these men the Engineers; she presumed that they were headed for a construction project on Koh Rong.

We spent another good hour on the runway. The flight attendant explained that the pilot was waiting for the tower to give him the green light. Then, without further notice, the plane took off. When it reached cruising altitude, the pilot announced that he was taking a longer route than usual to avoid a nearby thunderstorm. And after a few minutes, the flight attendant declared that food and drinks would not be served because of the anticipated turbulence.

I looked through the window. In fact, the plane was flying into a heavy dark cloud. Lightning was streaking all over the black sky. The passengers were silent but surely fearful. I looked at Sara, who forced a brief smile. "If this is the end, at least we will die together," she managed to whisper.

I squeezed her hand tightly. "Sara, it's not the end, I promise you."

Suddenly there was a loud noise, and the lights went off.

The plane started to swerve from left to right like a falling autumn leaf. The swerves were interrupted by several deep dives. Glassware and other objects went flying all over the cabin. A strong smell of coffee filled the air, and there were screams and cries from the passengers.

The flight attendant shouted from the front of the plane, "Prepare for a crash!"

Then there was silence.

The plane went through more frantic ups and downs and pitches from left to right. I signaled to Sara that she should lower her head and grab hold of her ankles, a crash position recommended by a flight attendant during one of my many business trips.

The plane must have touched down on rough terrain. It bounced and skidded over the ground, still at high speed. Then we heard the loud screech of the brakes as the Airbus came to a shuddering stop.

We were safe!

The passengers screamed, but this time they were screams of joy and relief. The pilot came out of the cockpit. He was pale and sweaty. But he wore a victorious smile. We all applauded.

After a few seconds, he said, "I don't know where we landed, but this was the only place I could find. Let's climb out and get a sense of where we are. But beware: when you leave the plane, keep in mind that it landed nose down."

After we all got out of the plane, the pilot made sure none of us was hurt. He also told us that the plane had no electrical power and that's why it didn't catch fire upon landing. The plane was safe for us to stay in—we could lie down in it and get some sleep or at least some rest. "In the morning, we'll have to find out more about this island," he said, then helped us all back to our seats.

Sara and I could not sleep. Holding hands, we thought about our extended family. Maybe there was hope that we would see them again after all.

Our faithful pilot left the plane early in the morning to explore our surroundings. After a few hours, he came back to check the supplies. Fortunately, we had enough food and water to survive a few days. The provisions stocked in the plane were meant for a much larger number of passengers.

He then chose people to help him survey the island. He asked the Nerds to check the forest and report back on what they found. He asked Mr. Commando to team up with him and follow a narrow trail to see where it led. He handed him a gun that pilots were allowed to carry when flying in that area. "You can use this better than I can," he said. "I'll take the hunting knife I keep in the cockpit for emergencies." He then asked the Engineers, who worked for Cambodia Angkor Air, to check the electrical system on the plane and assess the extent of the damage.

The four explorers put some food and water in their backpacks and left—the Nerds headed west, toward the forest, and the pilot and Mr. Commando headed east, toward the narrow trail.

Mr. and Mrs. Borshdbelt, Sara, and I got out of the plane to stretch our legs and look around. The Engineers were busy checking the electrical system.

We spent a long time with the Borshdbelts, a very interesting and gracious couple. His name was Mike and hers was Lea. Even in that desperate situation, they managed to make us smile. They liked to tease each other and tell funny stories. From time to time, we went into the plane to help ourselves to snacks and water. The Engineers, absorbed in their work, did not pay attention to us.

When night began to fall, the Nerds returned, tired and covered with sweat and mud. Their arms and legs were scratched and bleeding. We gave them water and let them rest before asking them about their explorations.

"The forest was very dense," they eventually told us, "with many venomous snakes and large lizards. We also saw pheasants and wild ducks."

Mike Borshdbelt could not resist making one of his witty remarks. "Great," he said. "Now we can hunt game and broaden our menu of peanuts and snacks."

"Yes, but you'll have to be ready to confront some larger animals, too," Mr. Nerd said. "We detected the presence of panthers and tigers, and we saw huge footprints in the dried mud next to a river. They looked like the prints of a large raptor."

"Forget the raptors. What if those panthers and tigers smell the delicious scent of human flesh here in the clearing?" asked Mike.

The question remained unanswered.

By that time, it was full dark, and we decided to get back in the plane. When we all had found our seats, one of the Engineers asked whether the pilot had returned. That's when we realized that he and Mr. Commando were still out there in the wilderness somewhere. "I hope they're staying safe," one of the Engineers said.

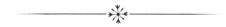

At sunrise the next morning, the whole group of us got off the plane and spread pillows and blankets on the ground so we could sit. This time the Engineers joined us. We picked at some peanuts, snacks, and water for breakfast as we talked about our situation and went over our options.

But by midmorning, we were seriously worried about the pilot and Mr. Commando. "Should I go and check on them?" asked the Engineer who seemed to be the leader of his group. He received a loud and unanimous "no" in response. We didn't want to fail by attrition. We were going to wait; after all, both men were strong and resilient. "They'll be here soon," I said, trying to reassure myself as well as everyone else.

Then, in the distance, we saw four shadows making their way toward us on the narrow trail. The lead Engineer jumped up, went into the plane, and came back with hammers, screwdrivers, and other tools that we could use to defend ourselves if necessary. He also carried a pair of binoculars.

Everyone chose a tool and waited. We decided to stay outside rather than go into the plane, where we felt we would be more vulnerable.

The shadows were getting closer. The lead Engineer looked through the binoculars, and after watching for a couple of minutes, he exclaimed, "I can see the pilot and our fellow passenger, but they are holding two women!" Our fear was replaced by intense curiosity.

When the group arrived in the clearing, Sara ran toward them and offered water. She then helped the two women lie down on a blanket.

We were all looking at the pilot waiting for an explanation. After drinking water and resting for a few minutes, he finally gave us a long and detailed account of their adventure.

After many hours of walking on the narrow trail, they spotted a building that looked like an old school some fifty yards ahead. It was guarded by four men dressed in military fatigues. They saw the head of a blond woman looking out one of the windows through a row of iron bars. They guessed that she was being held prisoner. Hiding behind a stand of trees, they took a long time to watch the four soldiers.

The men seemed bored. They passed a bottle back and forth and engaged in some desultory conversation.

The pilot and Mr. Commando sneaked through the forest toward the building, avoiding the trail so they wouldn't be seen. Approaching the building from the back, they looked around the perimeter and saw no other militants besides the four at the front. They then decided to free the woman.

They killed the four guards one by one—Mr. Commando with the gun and the pilot with his hunting knife.

They went inside the building, headed for the room where the woman was held prisoner. But suddenly two more militants came out of another room. The pilot and Mr. Commando fought them hand to hand in a desperate struggle for the militants' weapons. Eventually, Mr. Commando was able to kill one militant, and the pilot was able to badly wound the other. As he lay dying, the wounded militant told the pilot and Mr. Commando the truth.

There were around sixty of them, and they were actually pirates rather than militants. Most of them were survivors of the Cambodian genocide carried out by the Khmer Rouge. The pirates' aim was to attack the very wealthy people who cruised by the island in their hundred-million-dollar yachts. The pirates would chase the luxury vessels in motorboats and subdue them with machine guns, cannons, grenades, missile launchers, and other massively destructive weapons. Then the pirates would take possession of all the money, jewels, and desirable women on board the yachts and kill everyone else. The women they captured were sold into prostitution, often for substantial sums.

Finally, the wounded soldier succumbed to his injuries and died.

Mr. Commando and the pilot opened the door of the jail and found not one but two disheveled women dressed in dirty and torn rags, both blond and young. They were in bad condition. "Now their fate is tied with ours," the pilot concluded.

I was thinking that very soon the remaining fifty-four militants-pirates would realize what happened to their six comrades and would certainly come looking for us. Fifty-four of them, armed with deadly weapons, and thirteen of us, armed with only a hunting knife and a gun. The odds were not in our favor.

Mr. Nerd said, "Unfortunately, my news may be even worse. I told the group earlier that there is no way we can escape through the forest. It's too full of dangerous wild animals. We may as well stay here—the death will be less painful."

The pilot looked at the lead Engineer. "Any progress with the electrical system?"

"No good news there, either. We brainstormed and thought about a possible last resort. We're not optimistic about it, but we'll try it early in the morning. I wouldn't bet on it, though."

Mrs. Nerd, who hadn't talked too much until then, summarized what we were all thinking: "So there's nothing besides bad news?"

There was a long silence. Then Mike Borshdbelt announced, "I have good news—very good news. Last night I asked Lea, 'Did you send our charity pledge to the synagogue before we left?' She said that she did not. Then I asked if we had made our yearly donation to the Jewish Federation yet. 'Oh, no, I'm sorry—not yet,' she answered. 'One last question: Did you send the check for the Sim Shalom school's new building last week?' She had to admit that she didn't send that, either. So I gave her the biggest kiss I'd given her in more than sixty years."

"Why is that good news?" I asked.

"Because, my friend, they will find us!"

That drew a smile and even a chuckle or two from our sad and lugubrious group.

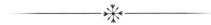

In the morning, though, we *did* have good news. The last-resort repair attempt the Engineers had come up with was successful. They managed to generate enough power to start the engines and even fly the plane for two hours.

Then it was up to the pilot to check the other systems and decide what to do. He walked around the plane with the lead Engineer and came back inside to announce his decision.

"I think I can get the plane to Koh Rong, our original destination," he said. "It's risky, but I think we can make it. I need a show of hands from those who agree to do it."

The pilot got a unanimous yes vote.

The flight was turbulent—the plane was chugging, pitching, rolling, and yawing—with plenty of sudden dives. But we were confident that our great pilot, our hero, would get us to our destination safely.

Upon arrival, we were greeted by several government officials, law enforcement personnel, and airline staff. Mike Borshdbelt, standing next to me, whispered, "Do you think these are the people who are waiting for our money?" He looked at me with a mischievous smile.

The next morning, Sara and I were at the beach, reclining under a large umbrella and looking out at the turquoise waters of the gulf.

"I think next year we should go back to the usual organized cruises," she said, and I agreed.

Yusha

*H*e was born in the intensive care unit of a hospital in a suburb of Izmir, Turkey.

His father and mother had a horrible accident while his father was frantically driving his pregnant wife to the hospital. Her water had broken while they were at home watching an Abbott and Costello movie. He hit a truck head-on; it was traveling at full speed, with no headlights on, directly into oncoming traffic.

His father and the truck driver were killed instantly. His pregnant mother was barely alive when she was driven in an ambulance to the hospital. The X-rays showed that she had internal hemorrhaging from various ruptured arteries in difficult-to-reach areas.

In intensive care, knowing she was going to die, she begged the doctors to save her baby. She told them, "If it's a boy, name him Yusha. If it's a girl, name her Naomi."

The doctors performed an immediate cesarian and delivered a beautiful baby boy. He was healthy except for his right hand, which had seven fingers. The doctor had seen a few polydactyl babies, but they all had six fingers, not seven. Otherwise, the boy was healthy and was expected to live a normal life.

Yusha's mother's breathing was getting shallower and more labored. Her vital signs were slowing. But she managed to extend her arms, expressing her desire to hold her baby before she died.

When Yusha was placed by her side, she touched his hands, ever so gently.

Suddenly, a jolt shook the bed, like an electric shock, and the lights dimmed. Yusha's mother's face came alive, and she opened her eyes wide. She shouted, "He has seven fingers—poor Yusha!"

Everyone in the room was astonished. Here was a woman who had been on death's door not moments before. "This is a miracle!" the supervising physician exclaimed.

The patient's vital signs were showing substantial improvement. The doctors could probably save her, but they had to move fast. The supervising physician asked his staff to transfer her to the operating room right away.

Yusha's father, Michalis, was Jewish, of Greek descent, and his mother, Ayse, was Muslim, of Turkish descent. They had both lost their families during the 1919–1922 war between Greece and Turkey and the massacres that followed. Greeks and Turks continued to hate each other even after the 1923 population exchange between the two nations, mandated by the Lausanne Treaty.

Michalis and Ayse worked in the same hospital, he as the director of the oncology department and she as its head nurse. They fell madly in love and got married in a civil ceremony officiated by a judge they both knew. Only members of the hospital staff attended.

During the years that followed, they ignored the hostile gossip and disapproving looks from people who couldn't understand their relationship. Their world was being together, loving each other, and doing things together. They also planned to expand their world with many children. But after more than ten years, that dream seemed impossible.

What surprise and immense joy they felt when Ayse discovered she was pregnant. After a few months, she and Michalis started making plans for the newcomer. They prepared a nursery, outfitting it with cheerful wallpaper, animal mobiles, and soft blankets. They even installed a loudspeaker system so sweet lullabies could play throughout the room.

One night after dinner, they chose names for the baby. It was a pleasant and frank discussion. They agreed that the names should be common to both Jewish and Islamic traditions. For a boy, Michalis wanted the Hebrew Yoshua but consented to Yusha, the equivalent in Arabic. For a girl, they chose Naomi, familiar in both languages.

Ayse spent a few more weeks in the hospital while Yusha was taken care of in the facility's nursery. She enjoyed having her baby with her for as many hours during the day as possible. His presence in her arms not only provided her with immense joy but also helped speed her recovery. "There's no better medicine for a mother than holding her baby," the doctor said.

Yusha was Ayse's main motivation for healing—she wanted to build a new life with her lovely boy. Ayse and Yusha left the hospital healthy and safe.

Ayse couldn't have survived the death of her beloved Michalis without Yusha, her miraculous son. She was going to face life with optimism and determination. She was going to be strong, resolute, and successful. And she would make sure that Yusha grew and thrived.

After going back to her old job as a nurse, she decided after a couple of years to open a business—a pharmacy, for which she qualified after attending night courses. Business was good. Her store was prosperous, with a growing base of satisfied customers who lauded her to their friends and neighbors. Ayse was happy, and Yusha was becoming a strong, confident, and handsome young man.

During his teenage years, he liked to go to his mother's store. He used to do his homework there and would help his mom by attending to customers. He knew which medicines were appropriate for all kinds of illnesses and pains. Customers loved him so much that they would come to the store and ask specifically for him.

Ayse was extremely happy about her son's popularity. It was good for business, good for him, and good for her. Maybe, when the time came, he would want to take over the store.

Ayse raised Yusha as a free spirit. She encouraged him from the sidelines, supporting him in his activities. She made sure he had a superb education. He attended the French school and the American Collegiate Institute, both reputed to be the best in Izmir. He then went on to the University of Cambridge, in England, where he would be exposed to a wide range of courses before deciding on a career.

But during his first years there, the students mocked him and harassed him. They even considered him a bad omen because of his seven fingers. In later years, however, his classmates began to befriend him and respect him. After all, he was one of the best students in his class as well as an outstanding athlete. He was even elected captain of the school's soccer team.

But what made him even more popular was his ability to cure pains and wounds that his teammates suffered during matches and practices. They all claimed that Yusha had magic hands.

One Friday night, he was alone in his dorm room. Most of his soccer teammates were attending a party in a room down the hall. The party was strictly hush-hush: verbal invitations were issued only to trusted players. Yusha suspected this was because his teammates were drinking and using drugs. Although he liked his teammates, he preferred to stay in his room and read. That night, it was Nietzsche's *Thus Spoke Zarathustra*.

Several hours later, Yusha was fast asleep when the door to his room suddenly opened and Henry, his roommate, rushed in, saying, "Our friend Charlie is dying, and nobody dares call for medical help!"

Yusha leaped out of bed and ran to the party, Henry following close behind. Charlie was lying on the floor, his teammates surrounding him, some holding glasses of water, others holding towels, but no one knowing what to do.

Yusha knelt down beside Charlie. His eyes were closed, his face was pale, and his lips were purple. He did not breathe and did not have a heartbeat. Yusha looked at the group and told them that Charlie needed immediate medical care. If he didn't get it, he would die.

The students vehemently refused to call for help. Henry turned to Yusha, frantic. "You take care of our wounds and pains when we play soccer—why don't you try to help Charlie now?"

Yusha thought Henry's request was ridiculous, but he couldn't very well turn it down. After all, he was their last resort. He asked the group to move back and leave space for Charlie in case he started to breathe again.

Yusha began CPR, with no response. He then put his hands on Charlie's head. Yusha instantly felt an electric shock all over his body. The lights dimmed, and Charlie opened his eyes.

Everyone in the room applauded and embraced Yusha. He had not only saved Charlie's life but also prevented the awful consequences they would have had to face if their alcohol and drug use had been discovered by Cambridge's faculty.

Yusha, however, knew that the CPR he tried did not save Charlie. It was only when he placed his hands on Charlie's head that his friend began to stir. Yusha knew from that moment on that he was a healer, but he had no idea where his healing power came from.

During Yusha's fourth and final year at Cambridge, he would sometimes accompany his soccer teammates to pubs on weekends when he had caught up on his schoolwork. On special occasions, they might go to a nightclub where they could meet female Cambridge students and dance with them.

It was during one such evening in a nightclub, when Yusha and his teammates were celebrating Henry's birthday, that he met Layla, a beautiful young woman with long black hair, large black eyes, and warm brown skin. Her father was Indian and her mother Irish. Her father owned a large trading company, and her mother taught English literature at Cambridge.

Yusha and Layla liked being together. They met often in the cafeteria and in the library at school, and on weekends they would go to the theater or to a pub, just the two of them. He told her about his background, about his parents' car accident, about being born in the intensive care unit, and about his mother's survival. He told Layla how nice and kind his mother was and how much he loved her.

Eventually, Yusha and Layla fell in love. She invited him for dinner at her house—her parents wanted to meet him. They were very welcoming, and he thought they liked him. However, he also detected, when he shook Layla's father's hand, a barely perceptible pulling away.

Yusha and Layla decided they would get engaged in Cambridge soon after graduation and then go to Izmir to meet Yusha's mother. He had already told Ayse about Layla in one of his frequent phone calls. But he and Layla made arrangements to stay in Cambridge for a while before traveling to Izmir—they needed to attend a party Layla's parents were planning for the purpose of announcing the engagement to their relatives and friends.

When Yusha took Layla to select her engagement ring, she picked a very simple and inexpensive one. But she looked at him and said, somewhat hesitantly, that she wanted something much more important from him than a ring.

"You know, Indians are very superstitious," she said. "It's a deeply ingrained part of their culture." She paused. Then she told him that her father had noticed that Yusha had seven fingers, a condition that Indians considered a sign of bad luck. Her father was afraid this would isolate them and invite tragedy.

Getting rid of his two extra fingers was something Yusha had not thought about before. But then again, he was always busy studying and playing soccer with his team.

"If that's all you're concerned about, I'll do it here, before we go to Izmir," he said. "Ask your father to find a qualified surgeon." Layla looked tremendously relieved. She was smiling as she headed home.

The surgery and the aftercare took a couple of weeks. By the time of the engagement celebration, Yusha's right hand was not different from the right hand of any other guest. Layla's happy father took Yusha by his arm and presented him to the large gathering. Yusha felt as if he had shaken hands hundreds of times.

Yusha and Layla decided to prolong their engagement for a year so they could analyze their options and make plans for the future. They wanted to wait until they had established secure and reliable careers before they got married. Layla wanted to be a pediatrician, a calling she was sure would provide her happiness and satisfaction.

Yusha was not as certain about a career. He loved science, arts, philosophy, history, and literature. He could study to become a teacher in any of these fields. He was also an excellent athlete and could easily have become a professional soccer player.

But he was also a realist, and he thought that the most practical thing to do was to become a pharmacist. It would probably be best for him, for Layla, and especially for his mom. Deep in his heart, he hoped Layla would love Izmir and would agree to practice medicine in that calmer and more peaceful city.

They arrived in Izmir on a sunny day in September. Ayse was delighted. She received Layla with open arms and a heart full of warmth and kindness. Like Yusha, she hoped Layla would like Izmir and agree to live there.

Yusha and Layla spent many months commuting back and forth between Izmir and Cambridge. Layla liked Izmir and told Yusha she would love to live there after completing her medical studies. She also supported the idea of his becoming a pharmacist, a job that would complement her own profession.

They spent time exploring the villages and small towns close to Izmir. They visited museums and some archaeological sites. Layla was particularly fascinated by Ephesus, an ancient Greek city near Izmir. She was dazzled by the remains of the Artemis Temple, which dated back to 550 BCE.

The couple also liked to spend some evenings in nightclubs, where they enjoyed dancing to Greco-Turkish folk music, especially the *zeibekiko*, Yusha's favorite. For Layla's birthday, he invited her and his mom to the most famous of these nightclubs. After dinner, when the musicians played a song he liked about love, he stood up and started dancing alone. The singer and the bouzouki players surrounded him. Layla, Ayse, and the other diners clapped along with the music. Ayse brought over a pile of dinner plates and broke them on the dance floor, a traditional practice during celebratory occasions. It was a nice evening.

One night, when Layla and Yusha were attending a performance of *Aida* at the Izmir State Opera, he felt his cell phone vibrate. As soon as he read the text, he told Layla they had to leave: his mother was in the hospital, in critical condition.

But when they left the theater, they encountered a horrible storm. Rain flooded the streets; thunder roared furiously, and lightning lit up the sky. Yusha drove to the hospital as fast as he dared, aware that he had to both control the car and, at the same time, control the fear and anxiety roiling through him.

Once they had entered the intensive care unit, Yusha realized that the situation was extremely serious. Ayse had a ruptured brain aneurysm. They operated immediately, but the brain was still bleeding. She was dying.

Yusha was desperate. He was a healer and had saved lives before; he had to save his mom now. He knelt on the floor beside the bed and put his hands on his mother's head. But he did not feel any electrical reaction like the ones he had felt on previous occasions. What happened? He realized that he must have lost his healing power when he had his fingers amputated in Cambridge.

He sobbed, tears flowing down his cheeks. In a last desperate attempt to save his mom, he joined his hands together and prayed in a mixture of Turkish, Greek, and English: "Please—let me save my mom. Please give me my healing power back just for this one time." He didn't know to whom he was addressing his appeal. It didn't matter—his voice was drowned out by the thunderstorm. He lowered his head onto his mom's arm, defeated and broken.

Then, after a few seconds, he felt an electrical jolt shaking his body. Lightning had struck the hospital.

And the light dimmed. He raised his head, looked at his mother, and smiled.

Acknowledgments

First and foremost, I want to thank my wonderful wife, Etty. She is my eternal love, my best friend, my strongest supporter, my source of inspiration, and the kindest mother and grandmother you could imagine. We have lived together for more than sixty-seven years—almost three-quarters of my life. But those years have been my happiest.

Etty was the first one to read each story after I had finished writing it. I would sit close to her on our couch while she read the stories aloud. From the sound of her laughter—and her screams of fright—I knew how much she liked them. She was my first beta reader while the book was in its infancy.

Thank you, Etty, *mon amour chéri*.

After a few stories had passed muster with Etty, I sent them to Jim Laricks, a longtime friend. He helped me by offering his comments on my memoir, so I know him to be sincere and objective, and I respect and value his opinion.

Jim liked my stories and thought they were all worthy of inclusion in the collection, to my great relief. He added, "Writing fiction at any age—let alone at ninety-three—is an achievement. These stories deserve exposure to the world."

Thank you, Jim.

Barbara Clark is my longtime editor and Etty's and my good friend. She knows a lot about our family, including our daughters, in-laws, and grandchildren. This book would have not seen the light of day without her involvement and encouragement. My only role was to write the stories. Barbara edited them, selected the pictures, and managed all the details with Archway.

Thank you, Barbara.

I would also like to extend my thanks to the courteous and capable professionals at Archway Publishing, particularly Deena Capron, who graciously answered all our questions and shepherded the book to the finish line.

Thank you, Deena.

Finally, thanks are due to my granddaughter Rachel, whose enthusiasm for the idea of my writing fiction propelled me to sit down and do something I had long dreamed of doing. I had fun along the way, and I hope my readers do, too.

About the Author

Jacques Sardas was born in Alexandria, Egypt, into a Jewish family of Greek and Turkish heritage. He grew up there and in Cairo, where he attended l'École Cattaui and l'École Sybile. An avid sportsman, Jacques was part of the Maccabi team that won the Egyptian national basketball championship in 1953.

In 1956, Jacques married Esther Pesso, whose family had roots in Yugoslavia and Greece. Before their first anniversary, he and Esther, who was pregnant with their first child, boarded a ship bound for São Paulo, Brazil. Two days after their arrival, in July of 1957, Jacques landed a job at a bank, and three months later, he was hired at Goodyear, where he would remain for more than thirty-three years. In São Paulo, he rose from file clerk to sales manager; he was then transferred to Paris, where he rose from sales director to president of Goodyear France. After a transfer to Akron, Ohio, he eventually became second-in-command of the entire corporation.

Jacques left Goodyear in 1991 and subsequently turned around several small manufacturing companies that were on the verge of bankruptcy. In 2008, he joined a leveraged buyout firm in New

York City as its vice-chairman and remained there until his retirement, in 2010. He and Esther live in Dallas, Texas, and have four children, eight grandchildren, and one great-grandchild. His previous book, *Without Return: Memoirs of an Egyptian Jew 1930–1957*, was called "compellingly and charmingly written" by the *Jerusalem Post*. *Taking Flight* is his first work of fiction.

Printed in the USA
CPSIA information can be obtained
at www.ICGtesting.com
CBHW042325010824
12556CB00060B/1636